GABRIEL HUNT

HUNT THROUGH NAPOLEON'S WEB

RAYMOND BENSON

A GABRIEL HUNT NOVEL

HUNT
THROUGH
NAPOLEON'S
WEB

TITAN BOOKS

Hunt Through Napoleon's Web
Print edition ISBN: 9781781169988
E-book edition ISBN: 9781781169995

Published by Titan Books
A division of Titan Publishing Group Ltd
144 Southwark Street, London SE1 0UP

First edition: August 2014
1 2 3 4 5 6 7 8 9 10

A CIP catalogue record for this title is available from the British Library.

Printed and bound in the United States.

www.huntforadventure.com

Did you enjoy this book?
We love to hear from our readers. Please email us at readerfeedback@titanemail.com or write to us at Reader Feedback at the above address.

To receive advance information, news, competitions, and exclusive offers online, please sign up for the Titan newsletter on our website
www.titanbooks.com

A GABRIEL HUNT NOVEL

HUNT THROUGH NAPOLEON'S WEB

1

GABRIEL HUNT'S GRIP ON HIS PICKAXE WAS SLIPPING.

He had been in worse scrapes before; it's just that he didn't particularly relish the thought of dying while caving for fun and practice. That would be an embarrassment. When it was truly his time to check out, Gabriel would much rather have his obituary say that he'd been eaten alive by an angry tiger or felled by gunshots from enemy assailants. Or old age. That wouldn't be so bad.

But to fall into a gaping pit because he had slipped on bat guano? *Preposterous!*

Gabriel called down to his friend and caving partner, "How you hanging, Manny?"

Horizontal and belly-down, Manuel Rodriguez dangled in mid-air on the end of the static nylon rope, fifteen feet below Gabriel's legs. His only hope for survival was Gabriel's grip on the pickaxe.

"Is that a joke, *amigo*?" Manny shouted. He was

trying to keep the terror out of his voice but wasn't doing a very good job.

It had happened quite innocently. Every two or three years, Gabriel made an excursion to one of various caves around the country so that he could hone his skills. His travels sometimes required that he perform a bit of spelunking—an outdated term, but Gabriel liked the sound of the word. It had a certain romance to it.

Dangling within an inch of one's life over a dark abyss, though, didn't have any romance to it at all.

Manny lived in New Mexico near Carlsbad Caverns National Park. Besides the exceptional landmark that was open to the public to tour on a daily basis, there were several other caverns in the park that were available only to experienced cavers. All it took to access them were a small fee and a license. Gabriel had done it many times, very often with Manny, a fifty-eight-year-old former ranger at the park and an expert spelunker.

They had been in one of the more "challenging" (as Manny had described it) caves for a little more than three hours when Gabriel and Manny—secured to each other by a fifteen-foot-long buddy rope—sat down to rest on a ledge above a black pit that supposedly led to a chamber of noteworthy formations. The hole was ninety-six feet to the bottom. They had come equipped with all the right gear. They each wore the necessary helmets, grubby clothing, knee and elbow pads, sturdy boots. Both men carried plenty of light sources and extra batteries, as well as water, snacks, trash bags, empty bottles in which to urinate, and a first aid kit. For the vertical descent, Manny had brought along an assortment of tools such as carabiners, rope, waist and chest harnesses, Petzl stops, rappel racks, handled ascenders, pitons, chocks, hammers, and a couple of pickaxes. The goal, however, was to accomplish the journey without damaging the cave at all. Hammering pitons into the rock face was to be avoided if possible. It was best to use non-invasive tools such as Spring-Loaded Camming Devices that wedged into already-existing cracks or in between stone protrusions. "Leave nothing but footprints" was the motto amongst serious cavers.

Gabriel had finished eating a power bar, coiled a long section of rope around his shoulder and back, and stood on the ledge to locate a convenient spot to install a chock or SLCD for what was called an SRT—Single Rope Technique—descent into the hole. The plan was that Manny would follow him, staying tethered to him throughout the excursion. But when Gabriel had stooped to examine a possible position, his boot slipped on something wet and slick. He slammed hard into the ledge, face down, and continued to slide across the slimy ridge until his body was falling through space. He must have plummeted twenty feet or so before he realized that he had pulled Manny off the ledge as well. Another dozen feet shot past before Gabriel swung the pickaxe that was, miraculously, still in his right hand. He chopped the rock face in front of him as hard as he could—and broke his fall. Hanging on to the axe's handle was another thing altogether. It had a ridged rubber grip and a lip at the bottom against which the side of his right hand collided painfully—but it was enough to enable him to hold on. He gripped the axe handle as tightly as he could with both hands, but already he could feel the strain in his fingers and arms. Making matters worse, his palms were moist from the sudden shock. And when Manny reached the end of the tether with a violent jerk, Gabriel really did damn near lose his grasp.

Then Gabriel was presented with the ultimate insult—he smelled the stuff he had slid across. It was all over the front of his pants and shirt.

Bat turd.

Gabriel winced, remembering a cave full of bats he'd found himself in half a year earlier in China. The smell was the same all over the world.

"This is the last time I go caving with you!" Manny called. His added weight dangling at the end of the line was slowly pulling Gabriel's shoulders from their sockets. "I'm a fool for letting you talk me into this again!"

Gabriel resorted to an old ploy—bravado could cover up genuine terror every time. "Come on, Manny," he yelled down, "you know you have to stay on top of the game. Sharpen your skills every now and then."

"I'm nearly sixty years old. I don't have anything left to sharpen."

Gabriel attempted to flex his arms and pull himself up, but with the extra load hanging below him it was impossible.

"What the hell do we do now?"

"Relax, Manny. I've got it under control."

In fact, Gabriel had no idea how to get out the predicament they were in. The rock face sloped inward in front of him, so there was no foothold within reach. The more serious problem was that he had only two hands, and they were busy holding on to the pickaxe for dear life.

After a few seconds of silence, Manny asked, "Anytime you want to start letting me know how you've got it under control is okay by me."

"Your light's still working, isn't it?"

Manny had a light affixed to his helmet. As he twisted slowly on the end of the line, the beam traced the pit's circumference.

"It's the only part of me that isn't failing," Manny answered. "My bowels are gonna be the next to go."

"Hold on, Manny. Take a look around you. Is there a ledge you'd be able to stand on if you could get to it?"

During his next 360-degree turn, Manny replied, "Yeah. Over on the other side. Behind you. But I can't reach it."

"All right. Let's see if we can get a little swing going, okay?"

"We need music for that, *amigo.*"

Sweat poured off Gabriel's forehead beneath his helmet, ran over his brows, and stung his eyes. Another problem on the rapidly expanding list.

"Shut up, Manny, and see if you can swing over to the ledge. Slow and easy. I'll try and get you started with my legs."

Gabriel managed to grip the taut tether with the insteps of his boots. He then strained to wiggle the rope enough to send some movement down to his partner. At the same time, Manny flapped his arms and legs as if he were trying to fly—anything to propel himself back and forth in the air.

"You look real graceful," Gabriel said through his teeth. It was becoming much more difficult to hold on.

"Not half as graceful as we're going to look when we're flat as tortillas on the bottom of the cave." Gabriel was glad that Manny was keeping his sense of humor. A good sign. But as his friend attempted the circus feat, the pickaxe started to squeak. As if it were about to come out of the rock. Gabriel needed to lessen the weight on his body in a big way. The sooner Manny got over to the ledge, the better.

He tugged on the rope with his legs some more and felt his partner's momentum increase a little. Manny was now a human pendulum, swaying feet first toward the target ledge, back and forth at a 20-degree angle… which soon increased to 30 degrees… and finally to 35 degrees. And then Manny's boot touched the edge of the stone outcropping.

"Almost there, Gabriel!"

The pickaxe creaked again.

Manny swung back to the ledge and came close enough to push off from it with his legs. The maneuver gave him more speed and force—but it also placed much more strain on Gabriel's wrists and the pickaxe. The metal lip at the bottom of the handle was deeply embedded in the flesh of Gabriel's hands. Then the axe slipped a few millimeters with a painful wrenching sound.

"One more push and I think I can make it!" Manny announced.

Gabriel was unable to speak. He simply closed his eyes and willed his partner over to the other side of the pit.

Anytime, Manny, anytime…

Manny returned to the ledge and pushed off hard. He swayed so far to Gabriel's side of the hole that he was able to touch the wall there. Then, on the way back to the ledge, he hurtled himself up and over—and fell onto the ledge with a *smack.*

"I made it!" Manny rolled and came to a sitting position. He panted for a few seconds and said, "Pardon me while I say a few Hail Marys."

The subtracted weight relieved the pressure on Gabriel's arms. He was now able to concentrate on the next problem at hand—saving himself. Manny was on the opposite side of the cave from where Gabriel hung and a couple of yards lower. The two men were connected by a fifteen-foot tether. Gabriel could simply let go, fall, and hope that Manny was able to pull him up to his ledge. But then they'd be stuck there. Most of the ascending equipment was back at the top, on Bat Guano Ridge.

No, wait.

He had some tools in his pack and in his trouser pockets. A few pitons. A couple of ascenders. A rappel rack.

Gabriel thought that if he could place an anchor in the rock face, he just might be able to attach his rope and a carabiner. He could then use the assembly to raise himself a few feet. Then he'd have to plant another… and another… all the way to the top. If he ran out, he could pull out one of the lower ones and re-use it. The trip would be slow going and painfully tedious… but it could be done.

Now if he could just grow another arm or two…

"So now what?" Manny called. His voice echoed in the well. "Dying from the fall would've been better than starving to death here."

"Don't be a pessimist, Manny," Gabriel growled. "I'll get us out of here. Trust me."

He took a deep breath. What he was about to do required concentration.

Gabriel squeezed the axe handle harder with his right hand… and let go with his left. Hanging by only one arm, he reached back with his free hand and dug into his pack. His fingers found one of the pouches— he hoped it was the correct one—and wormed them into it. He felt something cold, hard, and metallic. A piton! The angle was awkward, but he managed to grasp it. The next step was to pull it out of the pouch without… *dropping it…*

The piton fell into the darkness below.

He and Manny heard the clang when it hit bottom.

Gabriel rarely cursed, but he did so—loudly.

Let's try that again…

Still clinging to the handle with a very sore right hand, Gabriel reached back to the pack a second time. He dug into the pouch and took hold of another piton. This time he made sure he had it firmly in hand before removing it.

His right shoulder and upper arm were killing him. The strain was becoming unbearable.

To hell with not damaging the rock.

With the piton in his left hand, he eyed the rock face in front of him. A small crack ran diagonally across the limestone. Aiming as best as he could, Gabriel jabbed the piton's point into the crack. The first attempt only chipped some of the stone away. The second try created a small hole. With the third stab, the piton stuck.

Gabriel grabbed the axe handle with his left hand to relieve some of the tension on his right arm. Then, with his weakened but now free arm, he reached for the small hammer that hung on the right side of his belt. He succeeded in pulling it out of its sheath… but since the piton was to the left of his body, he now had to switch it to his other hand. He'd never be able to hammer it with his right hand.

Only one thing to do, and Gabriel knew he had only one shot to do it. There would be no second attempt.

Okay, the left hand is holding the axe. The right hand has the hammer. Let's do it…Ready?…One… two… THREE!

Gabriel tossed the hammer into the air and

grabbed the axe handle with his right hand while simultaneously releasing the handle with his left. The hammer had reached the top of its arc while he was making the exchange and was now plunging downward. Gabriel's left hand shot out and snatched the hammer out of midair as it fell.

He had to stop and breathe for a moment after that little stunt. Compared to it, hammering the piton into the limestone was easy.

Still using one hand, he unwrapped the rope from his shoulder and stuck an end in his mouth. He gripped it with his teeth, and then dug a carabiner out of a pocket. It was yet another awkward operation to secure the end of the rope to the 'biner with a bowline knot one-handed, but he did it. He then hooked the carabiner into the eye on the exterior end of the piton. The rope was now fixed and safe to use.

Then his cell phone rang.

"What the…?" He looked back at Manny. "You mean to tell me there's actually *service* down here?" Gabriel took hold of the rope with one hand and his legs, let go of the axe handle, and hung there, suspended.

The phone rang again.

"You're not gonna answer that, are you?" Manny asked.

Gabriel hated cell phones the same way he hated most modern technology—but that didn't stop him from feeling compelled to answer the thing when it rang. He fished it out of his trouser pocket and brought it to his ear.

"Hello?"

"Gabriel?"

"Michael?"

Gabriel immediately pictured his younger brother

sitting at his desk back in the luxury of his clean and comfortable New York office. He'd rarely envied his brother his stay-at-home life—but at this moment he came close.

"Are you sitting down?" Michael asked.

Gabriel grimaced. "Not precisely."

"It's Lucy, Gabriel."

The urgency in Michael's voice gave him pause.

Lucy—short for Lucifer—was the youngest sibling in the family. Their imaginative parents had named each child after one of the archangels in the Bible. It didn't seem to matter to them that their daughter would have to bear the ignominy of her moniker for the rest of her life. In an attempt at kindness, her brothers had called her Lucy, but in the years since she'd run away from home at age seventeen, she'd taken to calling herself "Cifer" instead. Pronounced like *cipher*, it made a fine name for the scofflaw computer hacker she'd turned herself into.

"What *about* Lucy?" Gabriel asked.

"Are you sitting down?"

"No, Michael, I'm not sitting down! Just tell me!"

"She's in terrible danger. You need to come back to New York as quickly as you can."

"How is she in danger?"

"It looks… it looks like she's been kidnapped."

He wasn't sure he'd heard Michael correctly. "Say that again?"

"She's been *kidnapped*."

"Are you serious?"

"Yes. And there's a ransom demand."

"How much do they want?"

"They don't want money, Gabriel. They want *you*."

2

GABRIEL TAPPED THE INTERCOM BUTTON OUTSIDE
the Hunt Foundation to announce his arrival,
unlocked the front door, pocketed his key, and
stepped into the foyer. The room was full of artwork,
antiquities displayed in glass cases, and brochures
about the organization for the rare occasions when
some museum curator or endowment representative
might visit the building. The rest of the ground floor
consisted of a dining room and kitchen, a small library
(the larger one was on the second floor), and one of
Michael's offices, where Gabriel was headed.

The brownstone, located on East 55th Street and
York Avenue, overlooked the East River and was
designated as a landmark. Ambrose and Cordelia
Hunt had lived and worked there, raised three children
there, and left it in trust to the Foundation in their wills,
which had been triggered when they'd vanished at
sea at the turn of the millennium. Michael, being the
responsible one in the family, was legally appointed

the manager of both the trust and the Foundation. That was perfectly fine with Gabriel. The less he had to deal with paperwork, taxes, endowments, grants, bills, and bureaucracy, the happier he was. He did find it handy to have money—you couldn't mount international expeditions the way he did without it—but he had no interest in the management of the various accounts and funds. Michael was a superb administrator and Gabriel knew such things were better off in his hands.

"There you are," Michael said as his brother stepped through the office door. The room was spacious, containing a pair of antique trestle tables, a gorgeous nineteenth-century mahogany desk, one wall lined floor-to-ceiling with filing cabinets, and two more lined similarly with packed bookshelves. What generally irritated Gabriel was how organized and uncluttered it was. And normally Michael's appearance matched the room's: tidy, neat, unruffled. At thirty-two he was quite the opposite of his older brother. Where Gabriel was six feet tall, broad-shouldered, ropy, and apt to show up with stains from smoke or grease or blood on his clothing, Michael was slight and bookish, wore wire-rimmed spectacles, and was never seen with a strand of his thinning, sandy hair out of place. Except for the thinning hair, he hadn't changed much since he was a boy. Gabriel had spent a fair portion of their childhood protecting Michael from neighborhood bullies, in neighborhoods all over the world, and not one of the encounters had discomposed Michael in the slightest.

But he was discomposed now.

"Talk to me," Gabriel said as he dropped into the chair in front of the desk.

Michael shook his head. "It doesn't look good.

I received an e-mail from an anonymous account. I printed it out." Michael handed it across the desk. Gabriel took it.

TO: MICHAEL HUNT—HUNT FOUNDATION

THE ALLIANCE OF THE PHARAOHS INFORMS YOU THAT WE HAVE LUCIFER HUNT. DO NOT CONTACT POLICE. DO NOT CONTACT FBI. YOUR SISTER WILL DIE IF YOU DO. WE REQUIRE THE SERVICES OF GABRIEL HUNT. HE SHALL MEET OUR REPRESENTATIVE ALONE, REPEAT ALONE, IN CAIRO.

The message went on to designate the time and place of a rendezvous three days in the future. At a stall in a public bazaar.

"After nine years, Gabriel!" Michael snatched the paper from Gabriel's hand and waved it in the air. "Nine years we don't hear from her, we don't know if she's alive or dead, and then this."

Actually, Gabriel knew, Michael *had* heard from her a few times—but only over the Internet, under her 'Cifer' pseudonym, which Michael assumed belonged to a thuggish, unsavory male who eked out a living skulking around the alleyways of the online underworld. It was an impression Gabriel had not disabused him of, even after learning the truth himself.

"My god, Gabriel. If they hurt her—"

"Do we know anything about this Alliance of the Pharaohs?" Gabriel asked.

"I spent the last twenty-four hours going through everything we have on Egypt. There's no mention of the group in any of the books we have, nothing in any of our files. The best I could do was a few hits on the Internet."

"And?"

Michael ran his fingers through his hair anxiously. "In the last two years, there have been two instances of Egyptian artifacts being stolen from major museums. The more recent was from the Louvre, in Paris. The French police attributed the crime to an *'Alliance Pharaonique.'* Another theft occurred in Istanbul a year earlier; Interpol isn't sure they're related, but the items stolen in both cases were from the same period. We're talking *ancient* Egypt—solid gold jewelry supposedly worn by Ramses II in Turkey, a goblet dating from Cleopatra's reign at the Louvre."

"That's all we've got?"

Michael turned his hands palm-up and the furrows on his forehead deepened.

"Great," Gabriel said. "So we know they like Egyptian artifacts, which we might have been able to guess from their name. And we know they were able to find Lucy, despite her best efforts to stay hidden." Gabriel didn't mention that he'd met with Lucy a handful of times over the past few years himself, once in this very building—no reason to make Michael feel worse than he already did. Besides, in each of those cases it had been Lucy who had found Gabriel, not the other way around. "What I don't understand is why they'd kidnap her just to get me to meet with them. Couldn't they just make a phone call? We take appointments, don't we?"

"They're criminals," Michael said. "I mean, if these *are* the same people responsible for those museum thefts. And if you're the sort of person who does that, you're probably perfectly comfortable kidnapping young women and probably don't like to do things through ordinary channels... Gabriel, *what are you doing?"*

Gabriel stopped stretching his arms. He'd been doing it unconsciously. "Sorry. I pulled some muscles yesterday in that cave. It's nothing. Just a little sore."

"I can imagine," Michael said, a censorious note creeping into his voice. "All I can say is thank goodness I was able to reach you down there. If you'd been out of range..."

"I thought I was," Gabriel said.

"Well," Michael said, "when you pay thirty thousand dollars for a cell phone, you do get something for your money."

"Thirty thousand? Really?" Gabriel said. "I'll try not to leave it in a cab."

"Gabriel, what are we going to do?" Michael threw the printout onto the desk, where it slid off onto the floor. He didn't pick it up. "I could never live with myself if they hurt her."

"Lucy's a tough customer," Gabriel said. "She can handle herself. She's probably giving them orders already."

"She's twenty-six years old," Michael said. "These men are killers."

"You didn't say anything about killing," Gabriel said.

"Two guards at the Louvre," Michael said. "One in Turkey." He paused, took a deep breath, let it out. "Decapitated."

There was a beat of silence.

"So I guess I'm going to Cairo," Gabriel said. Michael nodded miserably.

"I'll get her back," Gabriel said.

"She may be dead already," Michael said, his voice

dropping to a whisper.

Gabriel picked the sheet of paper up from the floor. "They pulled this stunt because they want something from me," he said. "As long as that's the case, she's alive."

THE DISCOVERERS LEAGUE WAS EMPTY AND QUIET that night.

Gabriel had calmed his brother by taking him to Andrei's place for a bite (Michael had protested that he wasn't hungry, but after his third glass of *divin* he was able to put away a plate of Andrei's *parjoale*). By the time Gabriel had seen Michael home and hopped a taxi to the building on East 70th Street, it was nearly midnight.

Hank, the elderly doorman who'd been with the club seemingly since its founding, greeted Gabriel warmly and handed him a bundle of mail that had collected since the last time Gabriel had been home. Gabriel got into the elevator and took it to the top floor of the building, where he kept a suite of rooms. The League's Board of Directors tolerated Gabriel's presence in the building because of who he was—the Hunt Foundation contributed generously each year—and because some of his higher-profile finds brought the organization the sort of attention that helped with their other fundraising. But their feelings about him were mixed. They'd had to spend a portion of the funds he donated on patching bullet holes in the walls and getting blood out of the upholstery, not to mentioned paying soaring insurance premiums, and some of the more staid directors complained that his exploits attracted less attention than notoriety. This discussion regularly consumed twenty or thirty minutes at the start of every board meeting; as the meeting room was directly below his apartment, Gabriel could sometimes hear the raised voices. But so far, no eviction notice had been slipped under the door, and the bullet holes kept getting repaired.

The two-bedroom suite was a little piece of paradise for Gabriel. Like most New York apartments, the place wasn't large, but it was everything he needed. The master bedroom had a four-poster and a dresser, though barely enough room to walk between the two. The guest bedroom was more of a catchall; it contained a lot of his "stuff," such as traveling gear and clothing. The living room was comfortably compact, dominated by a tiger skin rug (Gabriel had reluctantly been forced to shoot the animal when it had tried to eat him in India). The space had a lone couch, a desk, a few shelves of books. No computer, no television. Gabriel's prized piece of furniture was an antique Baldwin upright grand piano, manufactured in 1924 and as near to mint condition as one could get after nearly ninety years. He took better care of it than he did his own body—his sore arms attested to that.

Michael had arranged things so Gabriel could take the Foundation's private jet the following day. It beat having to deal with commercial airlines, and it also meant Gabriel could bring his Colt .45 pistol in his carry-on without anyone batting an eye. He hated being out of the country without it—so whenever possible he took the jet.

Michael had been delighted to put it at his disposal, but had been surprised when he'd insisted on flying into Nice, France rather than directly to Cairo. "Why there, Gabriel? I'd understand if you wanted to stop in Paris, talk to the people at the Louvre, but—"

"There's an Egyptologist I know," Gabriel had said

vaguely, "in Nice."

"Really?" Michael had said. "Who? Bourgogne? But no, he hasn't been at Antipolis since '08..."

"It's no one you know," Gabriel had said.

"An Egyptologist I don't know?"

"Yes, hard to believe isn't it," Gabriel had said, and changed the topic as quickly as he could.

There was no Egyptologist in Nice that Michael Hunt didn't know. Nor was there one Gabriel was going to meet. What there was in Nice was the last address Gabriel knew of for his sister. She'd been under house arrest for a time in Arezzo, Italy, and then somehow the charges wound up being dropped, or anyway that's what she'd claimed in her e-mail. The hasty change of countries was typical, and for all he knew she'd since abandoned the apartment in Nice. But since Nice was the last place he'd known her to be, Nice was the first place he had to go.

Gabriel showered, toweled off, and studied himself in the bathroom mirror. His slightly curly, midnight-black hair was in need of a cut, but that could wait. The various scars and bruises on his well-toned torso told many tales. He even remembered some of them.

Barefoot and bare-chested, Gabriel went to his kitchen, grabbed a bottle of Remy Martin, and poured himself a shot. He then sat on the piano bench and let his fingers roam absently over the keys. After a moment a melody emerged—"In the Still of the Night," one of his favorites. But somehow tonight it didn't fit his mood.

A framed photograph of the three Hunt children sat atop the piano. Gabriel had just turned sixteen when it was taken. That would make Michael ten and Lucy only four years old. She'd been an adorable little girl. Somewhere between four and fourteen, the adorable had faded and all sorts of simmering hostility had taken its place—but somehow never directed at Gabriel. Their parents, Michael, her classmates, her teachers... they'd all come in for their share of Lucy's particular brand of resentment. But Gabriel had always been spared. Maybe, he thought, it's because I wasn't around much.

By the time she'd run away—run away for good, Gabriel corrected himself; there'd been briefer disappearances before—she'd become quite the rebel, outspoken and independent and always looking for something to tear down. If she'd grown up in the sixties, he imagined Lucy would have found her way to Haight-Ashbury or onto Kesey's bus; in the seventies, she'd have been into punk rock. In fact, she *was* into punk rock, or at least the trappings that went with it. She had so many tattoos and piercings now that Gabriel had stopped counting them the last time he'd seen her.

He had to save her.

It was that simple. They'd taken her because of him, and now he had to find a way to get her back.

The first step toward which was to find her, period.

Which was not so simple.

Thinking about Lucy in Nice—or was she now in North Africa?—put him in mind of *Casablanca* and he found himself picking out the melody line of the *Marseillaise*.

Allons enfants de la Patrie
Le jour de gloire est arrivé!
Speaking of rebels.
Come, sons of France: the day of glory has arrived!

Followed by: *To arms, citizens! March!* Music to shed blood by.

They all were, anthems. Bombs bursting in air, and all that. Gabriel knew that at one point Napoleon Bonaparte, when he was Emperor of France, had banned the *Marseillaise*—but what had he replaced it with? A cheery tune called *Le Chant du Départ*. Gabriel picked it out on the keys and sang softly to himself.

La trompette guerrière
A sonné l'heure des combats…

The war trumpet has sounded the hour of battle.

Gabriel pulled the cover shut over the piano keys, downed his drink, and stood up.

Those bastards who took Lucy probably had an anthem of their own, some Egyptian version of the same bloody sentiments. War trumpets, battles, marching, marching.

Well.

They'd be singing a different tune soon.

3

THOUGH HE WASN'T MUCH FOR PARIS, GABRIEL WAS fond of the south of France and Nice was his favorite city in the country. Even under the present circumstances the sight of the countryside coming into view through the plane's windows brought a smile to his face.

Charlie dropped him off at Aéroport Nice Côte d'Azur and then flew the custom-built Bombardier Challenger CL-X to a hangar where it, and he, would stay until Gabriel needed them again. A man in his fifties, Charlie had been with the Foundation for years. Never said much; Gabriel had given up trying to engage the pilot in conversation long ago. But the man did his job well and took care of the plane as if it were his own, and what else did you need? Better to be in silent, safe hands than talkative, careless ones.

Gabriel made his way into the hilly, picturesque seaside town on his own. It didn't surprise him that Lucy had taken an apartment near the port; as she'd once told him, she found flat horizons comforting. On a quiet evening like this, the sight of the Mediterranean receding into the distance would've given her all the comfort she wanted.

The sun was setting as Gabriel located Lucy's building in the section known as Vieux Nice, which consisted of narrow, winding streets and old-town structures. The building was a crumbling, brick affair on a dimly lit lane near the water and the farmers market. It figured that Lucy would be living in a ramshackle place like this. She'd never had a taste for luxury. It was one of the things she'd spent her life rebelling against.

After checking to make sure there was no one around, Gabriel selected the thickest of a set of lock picks and used it to turn the heavy tumblers of the ground floor door lock. He replaced the pick inside the flat, leather money belt he wore beneath his shirt and let himself in. A set of creaking wooden stairs took him two flights up to the top floor. Number 303 was the door nearest the staircase. Gabriel reached for his picks again—but then he saw that the door was slightly ajar, the lock broken.

Moving slowly, he silently pushed the door open. The place was dark, heavy drapes drawn across the windows.

Except for one tiny spot of light moving on the other side of the room.

Gabriel felt along the wall beside the door and, when he found it, flicked the light switch.

A bare bulb went on overhead.

The first thing Gabriel noticed was that the apartment had been ransacked. Sofa cushions sporting deep slashes lay on the floor beside a pair of wooden desk drawers. Papers and debris littered the place.

The second thing he noticed was that the ransacking was still in progress. A woman with a penlight was standing by the desk, bent over its one remaining drawer. She looked up.

Gabriel shouted, "Hey!"

The woman quickly jumped away from the desk and darted through a doorway into the next room over. Gabriel leaped over the cushions in pursuit. The door to the other room slammed shut. Gabriel grabbed the knob—but as he did he heard the lock turn on the other side. He banged on the door with the side of his fist.

"Hey, open up! Who are you?" He repeated the question in French, adding, "I won't hurt you!"

Silence.

Well, he thought, *would you believe it if you were her?*

Raising one leg, he brought the heel of his boot down on the metal knob. It took two blows before the knob smashed and the door swung open.

The bedroom beyond was empty.

Gabriel went straight for the adjoining bathroom. No one in there. He pulled back the shower curtain. Nothing. He returned to the bedroom and opened the clothes closet. Just clothing. He swept his hands through the outfits hanging from the rod. There was no one hiding between or behind them. He dropped to his knees and looked under the bed. Just dust. He then went to the room's only window and opened the Venetian blinds. It was shut. There was a fire escape outside, but the window was locked from the inside. Unless she could move through solid walls, the woman couldn't have gone that way.

What the hell…? Where did she go?

Gabriel went back to the other room. She wasn't

there either. He skirted the mess on the floor and went into the small kitchen that was off to one side. He opened a cupboard and several pots and pans fell out.

He went back to the front door and looked out into the hall.

There *had* been a woman in the apartment, right?

He closed the door and surveyed the flat. There wasn't any other place she could have gone. A living room, a bedroom, a bathroom, and a kitchen. A coat closet by the door was open slightly. Gabriel yanked the doors the rest of the way and looked inside. She wasn't in there either.

Bizarre.

He recalled the brief glimpse he'd gotten of the woman. She was young—probably around Lucy's age, but it certainly wasn't Lucy. Mid-twenties, reddish hair down to her shoulders. About five-foot-seven. Wearing a black blouse and dark pants.

And very attractive. Nice figure, big blue eyes. Pouty mouth. It didn't take more than a glimpse for those sorts of things to register with Gabriel.

Lucy, meanwhile, stood maybe five-two in heels (not that she ever wore heels), and if her weight had ever tipped over into the triple digits he'd have been amazed.

Who was this woman? What was she doing searching through Lucy's things?

And how the hell had she gotten out of the apartment?

Just to make sure, Gabriel went through every room one more time. She wasn't there. The woman had vanished into thin air.

He took stock of the situation. The place was a mess—but it wasn't clear all the mess had been the handiwork of the woman he'd interrupted. Bits of electronic equipment were scattered all over the floor. A cheap flat-screen monitor lay face-down on the threadbare carpet. If they'd grabbed Lucy here, she wouldn't have gone without a fight; what he was seeing might have been the result.

A print of Jacques-Louis David's famous *Napoleon Crossing the Alps* hung over the desk. It had been slashed several times with something sharp. Gabriel moved closer to get a better look. Someone had also scrawled Arabic characters over one corner of the painting.

The Alliance of the Pharaohs? No way for Gabriel to know; he spoke only a few words of Arabic, mostly gutter slang he'd picked up on streets around the world, and he couldn't read the language.

Michael, on the other hand, could.

Gabriel whipped out his thirty-thousand-dollar cell phone, fumbled till he found the button to activate the camera, and snapped a close-up of the line of Arabic script. Instants later, the image was winging its way wirelessly back to New York. Modern technology had its uses, much as he hated to admit it.

Next Gabriel examined the clutter around the desk. A laptop computer was spread open on the floor, its spine bending the wrong way. It looked as if someone had stomped on it with a heavy boot.

Then he noticed the dark spot on the floor near the sofa. Gabriel moved closer and crouched.

Dried blood.

Was it Lucy's? Or had she wounded one of her assailants?

After canvassing the rest of the living room and kitchen, Gabriel returned to the bedroom. The double bed was unmade. A pair of pillows was on the floor and the sheets were in a torn heap. Bending to peer under the bed again, Gabriel spotted something on the far side. He got up, went around the bed, pushed it away from the wall and carefully lifted the object up.

It was half of a broken glass hypodermic syringe. The piece with the needle. There was some residue within the shattered barrel.

It either meant the kidnappers had used this on her or that Lucy had started shooting up for fun. Hell of day when "your sister's a junkie" is the better of your two options.

A sound from the hallway outside the apartment caught his attention. Gabriel heard heavy footsteps ascending the stairs. He rushed back to the front door and stepped out. Looking over the staircase rail, he could see all the way down to the ground floor.

Policemen. French policemen. Heading his way.

Gabriel looked around—he was already on the top floor, so there was no way out except down the stairs. He hurried back into the apartment, shut the front door as best he could, ran into the bedroom, and shut *that* door as best he could. Two broken locks meant two doors that wouldn't keep the *flics* out for long. He went to the window, unlocked it and raised it, just as the police thundered into the living room. Gabriel swung a leg over the sill and stepped out onto the fire escape landing. Steps led down to the landings on successive floors and a narrow ladder attached to the exterior wall led upwards, to the roof. Gabriel saw that two police vehicles were parked directly beneath him. Down was not an option.

He took the ladder two rungs at a time toward the roof. Just as he reached the top, he heard a shout from Lucy's window. The police.

Gabriel climbed over the short wall that surrounded

the roof and ran across the building. He reached the other side just as a uniformed officer appeared at the top of the ladder behind him.

"*Arrêt!*"

There was roughly a six foot gap between Gabriel and the adjacent building. He backed up, took a running start, and jumped, landing squarely on the next roof. As he continued to run, Gabriel glanced back to see that two other policemen had joined the first.

They must have felt daunted by the space between the buildings—the policemen halted at the edge of Lucy's roof. They shouted for him to stop but Gabriel kept going. He heard a gunshot go zipping past. He lunged for the edge of the building, grabbed hold of the top of the fire escape ladder, and hurled himself over the rim, landing on the narrow metal platform a few feet below. Beside him, a clothesline had been strung outside an apartment window and a variety of underwear hung from it: a man's undershirt with stains at the collar and sleeves, a frilly underwire bra, several pairs of shorts. Next to the clothesline a thick, rubber-jacketed coaxial cable ran from a hole next to the window, across a wide alley, over a wooden fence, and into a yard containing what looked and sounded like a generator of some kind.

Gabriel snatched the bra from the clothesline and slung it over the cable. Holding onto one strap with each hand, he pushed off the landing. The cable dropped precariously under his weight, but it was well anchored and didn't pull out of the wall. He slid down swiftly, dropping when he was a few feet above the ground, just before he would have slammed into the generator.

He took just a moment to catch his breath. The

policemen couldn't have seen him; they'd guess he'd gone down the fire escape and would be looking for him on the other side of the fence. For the time being, the safest thing for him to do was probably stay right here.

He thought so, anyway, until he heard a low, guttural growl behind him.

He turned his head to see two Doberman Pinschers. Staring at him. Baring their teeth.

Gabriel liked dogs well enough. He'd gotten along with plenty in his day, including some that hadn't liked anyone else. He smiled at these two, held his hand out, palm up.

The dogs continued to growl.

Then one of them barked. It must have been a signal, for both animals lunged at him. Gabriel leapt to his feet and ran, followed by the dogs' ferocious barking. He reached a tall tree on the far side of the yard, jumped, grabbed an overhanging branch, and pulled himself up just as a steel-trap jaw snapped at his legs. Gabriel continued to climb higher. One branch looked thick enough to support his weight and was long enough that its far end extended over the fence. He straddled the branch and crawled along it as the dogs barked and howled beneath him. The tree limb dipped as he crept toward its end. He could hear it beginning to creak. Gabriel kept moving. The dogs' jaws were snapping just a few feet away. The limb made a sickening cracking noise—and finally snapped when he was just short of the fence. Gabriel fell but managed to catch hold of the top of the fence. He heard the dogs' paws scrabbling in the dirt as they raced toward him, and then the sound stopped and he knew it meant they'd launched themselves through the air at him. With an enormous heave, he pulled himself over the fence, tumbling to the ground on the far side. Behind him, he heard the two dogs collide with the fence. They bayed with disappointment.

Gabriel bent to inspect his calf, to make sure he really hadn't been bitten. He hadn't felt a bite, but with the adrenaline coursing through him he wasn't sure he would have. But no—there were no bite marks, just a broad smear of dirt along one leg. The impact of the fall on his hands and arms was beginning to make itself felt, though, and it hurt like hell, all the worse for coming on top of the strain of his recent caving adventure.

On the other side of the fence, the animals continued making a racket. Gabriel thought it best to get out of there before the noise told the cops exactly where he was.

But where exactly was he?

An alley. One direction looked like a dead end, but the other looked like it emptied onto a fairly busy street some thirty yards away. Gabriel hurried toward the open end. As he neared it, a shiny red Peugeot 4007 screeched to a stop in front of him, blocking his escape.

The passenger door opened.

"Hurry. Get in."

The driver was a redhead in a low-cut black blouse displaying plenty of cleavage under a black leather jacket. Her lips weren't pouty at the moment, but there was no question who he was looking at. The woman from Lucy's apartment.

From somewhere behind the car came the sound of shouts, of running feet. Someone blew a whistle and, turning, Gabriel saw a policeman pointing a gloved finger in his direction.

"In or out?" the driver said, her French accent thick. "I am not remaining here."

He jumped in and slammed the door shut. The woman

pushed the pedal to the floor. With a squeal of burning rubber, the Peugeot merged recklessly into traffic. More whistles sounded behind them. The car shot through a red light and turned, barely missing a bus.

"Want to tell me who you are?" he said.

"Hush," the woman said. "Allow me to concentrate." She stared at the road intently, both hands gripping the wheel.

Gabriel heard a siren and glanced behind him. Sure enough, a police Renault was in pursuit, bubble lights flashing.

The woman made a sharp right turn into a one-way street—going the wrong way. Luckily, no other cars were in their path.

The Renault followed them. The woman shifted gears and sped faster down the street. As she reached the end, another vehicle started to turn into the lane, facing them. She leaned on the horn. The other driver panicked and drove off the road onto the sidewalk. The car hit a tree as the Peugeot zoomed past and out. She turned right and slipped into traffic with the police still hot on their tail.

They quickly came to a roundabout full of cars. The Peugeot spilled into the maelstrom, eliciting a cacophony of honking horns.

A taxi swerved in front of her, forcing the woman to pull the wheel sharply to the left, where a BMW in their way was moving much too slowly.

Gabriel braced himself with one hand against the dashboard.

But there was no collision.

He couldn't have described what she'd done if his life had depended on it—and he supposed it had. Somehow she had maneuvered through the circling traffic and was now exiting the roundabout. The police car was stuck in an inner lane, forced to make another trip around.

He looked over at her. She hadn't even broken a sweat.

"Nice driving," he said. He only knew one other woman—one other person, period—who could have pulled off a maneuver like that. "You're not Brazilian by any chance?"

"What? No," the woman said, and he could hear the dismay in her tone. "You cannot tell that I am French?"

"Just wondering," Gabriel said, and sat back. Wherever she was taking him, he at least felt confident they wouldn't crash getting there.

The woman headed down a side street and doused the headlights. Gabriel looked back to make sure they weren't being followed. He saw nothing behind them but darkness. The woman made a sharp left into an alley, slowed down, and finally came to a stop.

"So," she said. She reached into her jacket and pulled out a cigarette and a matchbook from an interior pocket.

Gabriel reached into his and pulled out his Colt .45. He pointed it at her.

"Now tell me who you are," he said. "And this better be good."

4

"PUT THAT AWAY," SHE SAID, LIGHTING HER CIGARETTE. "I am not your enemy. I just saved you from at least one night in jail. Maybe more."

Gabriel squinted at her. "That's swell. Who are you, and what were you doing in that apartment?"

"My name is Samantha Ficatier. I'm a friend of your sister's."

"You know who I am?"

"Of course. Cifer talked about you all the time. Gabriel Hunt, the famous explorer and adventurer, blah blah blah. Besides, you have her eyes." She nodded in the direction of the gun. "Now put that away." She smiled, took a long drag on her cigarette, held it before exhaling. "My friends," she said, "call me Sammi."

Gabriel lowered the Colt but didn't put it away. "How do you know Lucy?"

"Lucy!" she said. "She would be furious if I called

her that. You want to know where we met? We met in a history class at the university. We became good friends, took another course together. Then she dropped out."

"Wait, wait, wait." Gabriel shook his head. "Lucy went to a university? *What* university?"

"The University of Nice Sophia Antipolis. You didn't know?"

"No, I didn't know. When was this?"

"Two years ago."

He was flabbergasted. Lucy had never shown an interest in school before she'd run away. In learning, sure—she'd read constantly, tinkered with electronics. It certainly wasn't that she wasn't smart. In terms of raw intelligence she may have been the smartest of the three of them. But she'd had no interest in classes.

"What was she studying?"

"She didn't declare a focus of study, is that what you call it? She just wanted to take some classes in the Letters, Arts, and Social Sciences departments. She thought it would help her with her work."

"As a computer hacker?"

Sammi's smile broadened. "You know about that?"

"I do. She's pretty good at it, as I understand."

"Typical American understatement," Sammi said. "She is not 'pretty good.' She has no peer. She can enter any system, break passwords, you name it."

"They teach all that in the university here?"

"No," Sammi said. "That they do not teach. That you cannot learn. You are born with it, or you are not."

Gabriel sincerely doubted anyone was *born* with computer skills; if people were born that way now, wouldn't that mean they always had been? And god help the poor son of a bitch born with computer skills in 1706. Best he could do is grow up to be Ben Franklin.

"Look… Sammi, what do you know about what's happened to Lucy?"

The young woman raised her eyebrows. "What *has* happened?"

"You don't know?"

For the first time he saw a look of concern in her eyes. "No. Do you?"

Gabriel sat back in his seat. He watched to see how she would react.

"She's been kidnapped."

Sammi's eyes grew wide and she put her hand to her mouth. "My God! Please, no. Is this true?"

"Yes."

"Who did this?"

"First you tell me what you were doing in her apartment."

"I was… I was seeing if I could find out where she might be. Lucy and I were supposed to get together, the day before yesterday. She didn't show up, and that's not like her. She didn't answer her phone, and that's *really* not like her. Didn't return my messages. So I became worried. I finally came over… and well, I found it the way you did. The lock on the door was broken. The place was a shambles."

"It looked to me like you might have been the one who did all that."

She shook her head. "Not me. I was there only maybe ten minutes before you arrived."

"And you certainly didn't stay long after I got there. How did you get away?"

She shook her head and a mischievous grin played across her lips. "A good magician never reveals her secrets."

"And you're a good magician?"

"A very good magician."

"Is that like computer skills," Gabriel said, "something you're born with?"

Sammi shook her head again. "My father," she said. "He was a good magician first, and he taught me. All his tricks."

It took a moment for Gabriel to realize she meant it literally.

"Your father…?"

"Was a street performer, here in Nice. He specialized in escapes—like Houdini. I assisted him for many years when I was a girl. I would lock him in boxes, in crates, in cans, and he would get out. Eventually he taught me how to do them all. We even went to a tailor to have a miniature straitjacket made, of burlap, with silver buckles. I loved to wear it! He taught me how to escape from anything. Everything." She inhaled again and Gabriel watched the coal of her cigarette glow in the darkness of the car. "Until they put him in his very last box. From this box, he did not escape." She didn't say anything more for a little while. "I went on with it for a year or so by myself," she continued, "working the streets, doing tricks. I made some money; not a lot. People don't give money to street performers like they used to."

"So what did you do?" Gabriel said. "To make money."

"What I had to," Sammi said. "The skills my father taught me have such a lot of applications. Some more lucrative than others."

"Like getting in and out of apartments," Gabriel said.

Her shoulders lifted and fell. "In her way, it is what your sister does, too, don't fool yourself."

"So you're not going to tell me how you got out of her apartment?"

She stretched out an index finger, laid it across Gabriel's lips. "Secret," she said.

The touch startled him. There was an electric quality to it, and a quality of sudden intimacy, as though they'd known each other far longer than the length of a car ride.

She drew her finger back.

They watched each other for a bit.

"Are you hungry?" he asked finally.

"Ravenous."

"Thirsty?"

"Parched."

"You know of somewhere we can go? Get something to eat and drink?"

"You won't get my secrets that way, Gabriel Hunt. For just a glass of wine."

Gabriel smiled. "I'll take my chances."

SHE PARKED THE PEUGEOT NEAR THE WATERFRONT. There was no sign of the police. They walked to a sidewalk café that was open late. The crowd inside was young, mostly college-age, and loud; Gabriel and Sammi took an outside table where they could talk privately. She ordered them a plate of *socca*, a Niçois specialty consisting of a thin layer of chick-pea flour and olive oil batter fried on a griddle, as well as a dish of stuffed vegetables. Gabriel consented to the waiter's offer to bring a bottle of the house's red wine.

The table was lit by a pair of candles in tiny glass holders. Gabriel couldn't help but admire Sammi's features in the flickering light, the play of shadow over her tanned skin (so much darker than most redheads he knew—and yet the red looked natural). Her eyes were an even brighter blue than he remembered from his first glimpse of her in the apartment. She wore a small medallion of some kind on a gold chain around her neck, and as she leaned toward him it dangled in the inviting darkness between her peach-shaped breasts.

"What is that?" he asked, indicating the medallion.

"This?" She lifted the chain with one finger, let the piece dangle in the light of the flame. "This is nothing, really. I wear it for sentimental reasons. It once belonged to my mother, who is no longer with us."

"It looks old."

"More than two hundred years," she said. "It's a French coin from around 1800. A franc. An old franc, from Napoleon's time."

Gabriel thought about the print of Napoleon on the wall of Lucy's apartment, defaced by blade and marker. The old boy seemed to be turning up everywhere. But that was what it meant to come to France, of course. Two centuries later, his influence was still palpable.

"Speaking of Napoleon, do you know why my sister had that print up on her wall?" Gabriel asked. "Had she developed an interest in history?"

"Cifer? No. History was my specialty, not hers. I gave her the print for her birthday. I told her once she reminded me of Napoleon. Small, but very, very brilliant."

"I'm surprised I never noticed the resemblance," Gabriel said.

"Well," Sammi said, in a tone of consolation, "you are not French."

The wine arrived then, and Gabriel went through the performance of sniffing the cork and swirling the wine and satisfying the waiter by pronouncing it good enough. When the waiter left, Sammi took one swallow and burst out laughing. "It's awful!"

"It is," Gabriel said. "Worst I've had in years."

"But, but—why didn't you send it back?"

"I'm not here for the wine," he said.

They found each other's eyes, and neither looked away for some time.

"Can you tell me," Sammi said, "is Cifer in serious danger?"

"I don't know," Gabriel said. "I hope not. But she may be. A group calling themselves the Alliance of the Pharaohs claims to have kidnapped her. Have you ever heard of them?"

"God in heaven," she said. "I remember our Mediterranean History professor mentioning them. That's the class Lucy and I were in together."

"Really? Your professor mentioned them? My brother Michael—he has two degrees in history, and he'd never heard of them."

"That's because they're not historical," Sammi said, "they're entirely modern. A sect operating in present-day Egypt. Very radical. Made up of intensely passionate Egyptian nationalists. Among other things, their aim is to repatriate any Egyptian artifacts and treasures they see as having been stolen by other countries."

"Stolen's a bit strong," Gabriel said. "Most of what's in museums was legally obtained."

"Most is not all," Sammi said, "and 'legally obtained' is in the eye of the beholder. And in their eyes a great wrong has been committed. One they feel calls for revenge."

"The thefts in Istanbul—"

"And from the Louvre, yes. We discussed them in class. Our professor didn't approve of the tactic—"

"By 'tactic' you mean beheading the security guards?"

"—but he seemed sympathetic to the desire for Egypt to have her artifacts back. But then, he was Egyptian himself."

"Do you suppose he'd be willing to talk to me? I'd like to know more about this group before I meet with them."

"I wouldn't know how to contact him—he was a visiting professor only, he went back to Egypt at the end of the semester. But Gabriel," she said, reaching out and taking hold of his hand, "surely you are not going to meet with members of this group. Of all people, not you."

"Why 'of all people'?" Gabriel said.

"For heaven's sake, what are you known for? How many precious artifacts have you taken out of Egypt and her neighbors and brought back to the United States? If this group has two enemies, it must be you and Howard Carter. And Howard Carter they can no longer kill."

"I may not be quite as easy to kill as they think," Gabriel said.

Sammi's voice shook when she spoke. "But don't you see? That is why they took Cifer. With her life in the balance, how could you dare to fight them?"

"I'll think of something," Gabriel said, with more confidence than he felt. "Listen, did you find anything when you searched Lucy's apartment? Anything that might be helpful?"

"Just this." She reached into her purse and pulled out a small plastic bag. It contained the other half of the broken glass syringe, the half with the plunger. "It was on the floor in the bedroom."

Gabriel nodded. "I found the other half behind the

bed. Can I take it Lucy isn't a drug user?"

"Hardly! She doesn't even like to drink very much."

"Then it must have been the kidnappers," Gabriel said. "Some sort of knock-out drug, maybe."

"We'll find out," Sammi said. "Before I picked you up, I called a man I know who has a pharmacy and he agreed to run some tests. In fact—" She took out her cell phone and looked at the clock on its display. "We'd better get going, it's almost eleven."

"He stays open till eleven?"

"Jean? No, he closes at seven; eight on weekends. But that's for ordinary customers. For me... he'll make an exception."

Gabriel tried to read the expression he saw in her eyes. "Sounds like he might prefer if I stayed in the car," he said.

"I am sure he would," Sammi said. "But I would not." And she squeezed his hand once more.

5

LA PHARMACIE WAS CLOSED, OF COURSE, BUT SAMMI
rang the bell and after a moment, a light went on in the
back. Someone came to the door, flicked a switch, and
the metal security gate rolled up slowly. Then the door
swung open.

The chemist was a man in his forties, the sort you
could tell had been fit once but hadn't kept at it, so
that now he was glad to have a bulky pharmacy apron
to hide behind. He was mostly bald and had a pair
of glasses hanging on a chain around his neck. He
smiled warmly at Sammi, greeted her in French, and,
wrapping his arms around her, kissed her on both
cheeks. Her body language revealed all—to Gabriel.
The chemist seemed oblivious to the discomfort she
showed in his embrace.

"Jean, I'd like you to meet my friend from America,
Gabriel Hunt," she said after sliding out of his grip
with a facility that would have made her late father

proud. "Gabriel, this is Jean."

The chemist's smile vanished when he shook Gabriel's hand. "I am pleased to meet you," Jean said, sounding the farthest thing from pleased.

"Likewise," Gabriel replied. "Thank you for seeing us so late."

The man sniffed. "For my Samantha, anything. Come this way."

They followed him through the shop and into the back, turning down a corridor and passing through it into a windowless room that held Jean's lab and workspace. It was filled with mortars and pestles, measuring instruments, test tubes, beakers, and other instruments of his trade. Through the open doorway to an adjoining supply room Gabriel could see metal shelves piled high with containers of prescription drugs. An older woman in a caftan and headscarf stood by a deep metal sink in the corner of the room, rinsing out glassware and setting each piece mouth-down on a rack to dry.

"Kasha," Jean said. He had to repeat it before the woman looked up. "You can finish that later. Later. Thank you." The woman turned off the water, dried her hands, and stepped out.

"So: what can I do for you this evening, my dear?" Jean asked.

Sammi pulled out the plastic bag and handed it to him. "We need to know what was in this syringe."

"'We,'" Jean said, frowning. Or perhaps he had only said, "*Oui*," Gabriel wasn't sure.

The chemist opened the bag and carefully removed the broken hypodermic, then slid his glasses onto his nose. He muttered something that Gabriel didn't catch.

"Excuse me?"

Jean looked down his nose at the American. "I said if there is still residue in it then it shouldn't be a problem. However, there is none visible to the naked eye. Give me a moment. Why don't you have a seat in my office, Mister Hunt?" He pointed to another door across the hall, next to a flight of stairs that led to the second floor. "Kasha can make you some tea."

"Thank you, Jean," Sammi said, "that'll be lovely. Come." And she took Gabriel's arm before Jean could protest that he hadn't mean for *both* of them to go.

His office was a small room dominated by a large metal desk and a ceiling fixture set up to direct its light at the framed diploma on the wall. Gabriel glanced at it briefly, then sat in one of the two guest chairs. "So," he said. "How well do you and Jean know each other?"

"Not as well as he would like," Sammi said.

"That much is clear."

"He's not a bad guy," Sammi said, her voice dropping to a whisper, "he just doesn't understand that I'm not interested in—" She stopped when Kasha appeared in the door with a tray in her hands. There were two bone china cups and a steaming teapot. "Thank you, Kasha, that smells wonderful."

"It is *touareg*," Kasha said softly. "I recall how you liked it last time."

It did smell good, the steam thick and minty, with an undertone of wormwood. It reminded Gabriel of the tea he'd had in Morocco while hiding out from two rather aggressive members of the Royal Gendarmerie. As he'd been unable to leave his host's cellar for nine days, he'd had plenty of time for drinking tea. It had been the only good part of that whole incident.

Gabriel stood to take the tray from Kasha, but his jacket pocket began buzzing before he could. "Excuse me," he said, and fished out his phone. Sammi took the tray from her instead. "It's Michael," Gabriel said. "My brother. I sent him a picture of the writing on the print, the Arabic characters. I figured he'd be able to read them."

"Was he?" Sammi poured them each a cup of tea, then handed the pot and tray back to Kasha.

"Take a look." He swung the phone's screen in her direction and tapped the screen to enlarge the image. Michael had annotated the photo in his meticulous handwriting.

"'This is the thief who resides in hell,'" she read. "What does that mean?"

Gabriel saw that Kasha also was looking at the screen. Her knuckles were white where she clutched the handles of the tray. "Do *you* know what it means?" he asked her.

"No sir," she said. If possible, her voice had gotten even softer. "I do not know. But surely it... it cannot mean anything good. Pardon me." And she carried the tray out.

"Do you think it refers to Lucy?" Gabriel said.

"More likely it would refer to the man in the picture," Sammi said. "Don't you think? If this is the Alliance of the Pharaohs, well... perhaps he is no Howard Carter or Gabriel Hunt, but Napoleon certainly took his fair share of artifacts out of Egypt. And we're not talking 'legally obtained,' either."

"But they can't think any of those artifacts might be in Lucy's possession," Gabriel said. "That makes no sense."

"How about in your possession? Or your Foundation's?"

Gabriel shook his head. "Nothing. Of Napoleon's? Absolutely nothing."

"Perhaps," Sammi said, "it's not something you have. Perhaps it is something they want, and they think you can get it for them."

"Why would they...?" But Gabriel didn't finish the sentence. The answer was obvious. Why would they think Gabriel Hunt could find something for them—some ancient treasure, say, that had once been stolen from Egypt by Napoleon Bonaparte and lost over the two centuries since? Because that's what Gabriel Hunt did. And the price of his worldwide fame—notoriety, if you will—was that everyone knew it.

"It's possible," he conceded. "I guess I'll find out soon enough."

"We both will," Sammi said. "As soon as we get to Cairo."

"*We?*" Gabriel said—and he hoped she knew he wasn't saying "*Oui.*" "*We* are not going to Cairo. I am going to Cairo; you are staying right here, where you're—"

"Where I'm what," Sammi said, "safe? Like your sister was safe? While you go off to Cairo by yourself and get yourself killed, and Cifer too, while you're at it? Not on your life."

"No point in all three of us getting killed," Gabriel said.

"How about all three of us surviving? That's more the sort of thing I had in mind."

"You wouldn't be—" Gabriel began, but she raised an index finger curtly to silence him.

"You are not about to say, I hope, that I would not be able to take care of myself," Sammi said, "that you would have to watch out for me—you are not about to say something along those lines, are you, not after I was the one who rescued you from the police, not to mention deftly escaping from your clutches back at your sister's apartment and doing so without your having the faintest notion of how I accomplished it? Surely, Mister Hunt, you're not about to suggest that I would need your protection?" And she smiled at him through savagely clenched teeth.

"Of course not," Gabriel said.

"Good."

"So what were you going to say?"

Gabriel paused. "Nothing important."

"I thought so," Sammi said, crossing her arms over her chest.

Well, Gabriel thought, *if she wants to come, let her come*. A former street rat like this… if he tried to stop her she'd probably just follow him anyway. And who knows what sort of trouble she'd get into then.

"You can come," he said, and this time it was *his* index finger that rose warningly, "but only if you follow my lead. Do you understand?"

Jean chose that moment to enter the office. "I have the results," he announced.

Sammi and Gabriel looked at each other.

"After you," Sammi said.

THE CHEMIST LED THEM BACK TO HIS LAB ROOM AND pointed toward a row of stoppered test tubes. Next to them, the flame of a Bunsen burner tickled the bottom of a flask. "You were correct, *chérie*," Jean said, facing Sammi and turning his shoulder to Gabriel. "There were still some traces of a chemical compound in the hypodermic. Sodium pentothal."

"Isn't that what they use to put people to sleep?" she asked.

"It can be. It is commonly employed as a component for the induction phase of general anesthesia. In the past it was known as a truth serum."

"Pentothal could also be used to make someone compliant, right?" Gabriel asked. "Someone who was putting up resistance?"

Jean glanced back at him over his shoulder. "Yes, in small doses. A large dose might be fatal." He turned back to Sammi. "Now, my dear, how can I be of further help? Can you tell me where you found this? Who was injected with it? How it came to be shattered…?"

"I'm sorry, Jean," she said. "I can't. Not yet. I will tell you more when I can, I promise."

"But this could be quite serious," Jean said. "In a case like this, I really ought to notify the authorities—"

Sammi put a hand on one of his meaty wrists. "Don't."

"But if you do not tell me at least a little about what you are—"

"For my sake, please."

Jean considered this, then heaved a mighty sigh. He took his glasses off and let them hang against his chest. "For you, Samantha. Anything."

She leaned in and kissed him on the cheek. The man's bald head turned red and he stammered something to her in French that Gabriel didn't catch. Sammi just laughed and said, "Jean!"

"Until next time," Jean said. And turning to Gabriel: "*Monsieur.*"

His tone was as frigid as the inside of an ice chest, but Gabriel ignored it. The man's earlier words were still echoing in his head. *A large dose might be fatal.*

* * *

KASHA WATCHED GABRIEL AND SAMMI LEAVE THE shop from her second floor bedroom window. When they were out of sight, she picked up the telephone beside the bed and dialed a number in Morocco. She spoke a few sentences in Arabic, waited until the man on the other end acknowledged her report, and then hung up.

6

THE MERE NAME OF CAIRO, ONE OF THE OLDEST CITIES in the world, immediately conjures up images of pyramids, mosques, camels, and sand dunes. In reality, it is a booming modern metropolis of nearly seven million people.

But Gabriel knew if you looked you could still find traces of the Cairo that once was, especially in the section of the city known as Old Cairo. Once called Coptic Cairo, it was a center of early Christianity until the Islamic era. The sights and smells and sounds of Old Cairo combined to provide visitors with a picture to rival any fantasy they might have of the fabled city.

It was half past noon when Gabriel and Sammi arrived. The sun was blazing in the sky and the streets in the center of the city were packed with people and automobiles. The cars dwindled as they got to the narrower streets of Old Cairo, where foot traffic was the norm. Gabriel's meeting with the Alliance of the

Pharaohs wasn't until one o'clock. He and Sammi sat in a café on the border of the famed Khan el-Khalili, the bazaar that dated back to the fourteenth century. They made a quick meal of *kushari*, a heavily spiced blend of rice, lentils, and macaroni smothered in a sauce of garlic and vinegar.

"Do you know how to find the stall where you're supposed to meet them?" Sammi asked as she studied a pocket map of the market they'd picked up.

He pointed to a spot on the maze of streets. "Right there."

"All right," she said. "And then what?"

"I imagine they'll want to go someplace else to talk. It won't be out in the open, you can be sure of that." Gabriel traced his finger along one crooked street. "Possibly here or here. One of the places tourists don't go. Which will make it difficult for you to follow us without being noticed."

"Don't worry about me," Sammi said. "I know a thing or two about getting around without being seen. I did a pickpocket act with my father—"

"I'm sure you were terrific at it," Gabriel said, "in Nice, where you speak the language and redheads aren't so uncommon. Here it won't be as easy."

As he spoke, she dug through the shoulder bag she'd hung from the corner of her chair. She pulled out a headscarf similar to the one Kasha had worn. In seconds, every lock of her hair was neatly tucked away beneath it. "Don't worry about me," she repeated. "You just take care of yourself."

Gabriel took the cell phone from his jacket pocket and turned it off. "I don't need this thing going off while I'm meeting with them."

She took it out of his hands, turned it back on again.

"What are you doing?"

She waited for the screen to light up and then pressed a button on the side. A loud tone was followed by a quieter one, then a quieter one still, and finally no sound at all. "Just turn the ringer off. That way I can at least send you text messages if I need to."

"How would I know you've sent one?"

"Look at it once in a while," she said. "If I've sent one, you'll see it."

Gabriel didn't argue, just tucked the phone back in his inside pocket, where it nestled next to his Zippo lighter.

"Suppose they take you inside a building," Sammi said. "How long do I give you?"

Gabriel thought about it. "Two hours. If I'm not out by then, I want you to go back to the hotel and call Michael. You have his number, right?"

"You've given it to me twice."

"Well, use it. If anything goes wrong. I don't want you coming in after me by yourself."

Sammi gave him an exasperated look.

"I mean it," he said. "I don't want you getting hurt, or worse."

"Neither do I," Sammi said, "believe me. There are few things I like less."

"Good." Gabriel looked at his watch and got to his feet. "Now remember, you follow from a *distance*. Understand?"

"It's what I've got these for." She pulled the pair of binoculars they'd bought on the way into the city from her bag and slung them around her neck. "Or does that make me look too much like a tourist?"

It did make her look like a tourist. But he thought that was a good thing, on the whole. They were less likely to do anything to a tourist. "You look fine," he said.

Sammi took his hand, gave it a squeeze. "Be careful, Gabriel."

"Always," he said. He walked out of the café, crossed the busy street, and entered the bazaar. Sammi gave him a half-minute head start, then gathered her things, left a few bills on the table, and followed him.

GABRIEL WALKED PURPOSEFULLY THROUGH THE twisty streets of the souk. On either side, an endless variety of shops and food stalls advertised wares both ancient and modern, the owners calling out to him as he passed and urging him to come and buy. Clothing, jewelry, spices, perfumes—if you knew what you were looking at, some authentic bargains could be had. You even came across the occasional rare piece of real value. Invariably stolen, of course, and bound to be confiscated if you tried to carry it out through Customs at the airport. At another time, Gabriel might have enjoyed exploring a bit, maybe even haggling with a vendor or two (nothing here was for sale at fixed prices). But that would have to wait for his next visit. If he had a next visit.

He found the location he was looking for, a store labeled with a sign in Arabic and English. The English portion identified it as *Jumoke's*. The store was built into the ground floor of a two-story building. Elaborately patterned carpets hung from poles outside the shop and also served as an awning. It was one of the larger venues in the souk.

Gabriel stopped by the entrance and pretended to be interested in one of the carpets. He casually glanced back the way he'd come, but there was no sign of Sammi. That was a good thing. After a moment, a short Egyptian man approached him from the back of the store.

"Good afternoon, sir. You have a fine eye—that is our most beautiful carpet."

"It's very nice," Gabriel said.

"You want it? I make you a good deal." The man's eyes glittered.

"I'm afraid not," Gabriel said. "I'm just looking."

Gabriel felt a hand land on his shoulder from behind. "Do not turn around, Mister Hunt." The hand moved, frisking him. First one side, then the other. He felt his Colt being lifted out of its holster. The Egyptian in front of him had an apologetic expression on his face.

"I was *this* close to buying it, too," Gabriel said.

The Egyptian shrugged. "You still can. We ship."

But by then the frisking had ceased and Gabriel had other things to focus on. A man walked around from behind him, one hand extended. He was very tall, a few inches past Gabriel's own six feet. He wore a lightweight white suit and a fez. His skin was olive-colored, his eyes dark brown and piercing. Beneath his lower lip he sported a thick goatee. Gabriel figured him to be in his fifties.

"My name is Amun," the man said. "Thank you for being so punctual, Mister Hunt. You are right on time." The man's English was accented, but mildly; it sounded smooth and cultured, as though many hours of practice had gone into polishing it. He might have been an actor or a politician.

"You're with the Alliance of the Pharaohs?" Gabriel asked.

"I am." He gestured over Gabriel's shoulder and Gabriel turned his head to look. Behind him stood a much larger man, not so much in height as in bulk. He was dressed in a suit as well, but no fez.

"This is Kemnebi," Amun said. "He is my assistant."

"What does he type," Gabriel said, "ninety words a minute?"

Amun chuckled. His offered hand having gone unshaken this long, he let it fall to his side. "Why don't the three of us go inside this shop and have a talk?"

"I'm not going anywhere until I know that Lucy is all right," Gabriel said.

"You have my word, Mister Hunt."

"And you have my sister," Gabriel said. "Your word means very little to me."

"You wish to talk to her?" Amun said.

"Yes."

"Come inside. We will get her on the phone. It is more private, don't you think?"

"You can get her on the phone right now."

Amun smiled slightly. "Out here?"

"Out here."

"Very well." Amun removed a cell phone from his pocket and keyed in a number. He spoke Arabic to someone on the other end. After a pause, he handed the phone to Gabriel.

"...hello?" It was a woman's voice. She sounded as if she'd just been awakened from a deep sleep. It could have been Lucy. Or not.

"Lucy?" he said cautiously. "It's Gabriel."

"Gabriel? *Gabriel!* Where are you?" She still sounded half-asleep—but it was her.

"Are you all right?" he said. "Have they hurt you?"

"I'm okay. I'm just... sleepy. The bastards gave me—" But her voice was cut off.

"Lucy? *Lucy!*"

Amun held out his hand for the phone. Gabriel angrily slapped it into the man's palm. The Egyptian held it to his ear, spoke a few more words in Arabic, and then hung up.

"As you can hear, your sister is alive and well. My word is good, Mister Hunt."

"She's alive," Gabriel conceded. "She didn't sound well. What have you pumped her full of?"

"Nothing worse than people her age pump themselves full of every day. It's probably a good deal safer, in fact, and less unpleasant when it wears off." The man shook his head. "Please understand, we had to calm her down, or she would have hurt herself trying to get away. She might have hurt others as well. Believe me, it is better this way."

"I ought to wring your neck right here."

"You could try to do that, Mister Hunt. But Kemnebi would prevent it, and if he failed, you have my word that your sister would be dead within five minutes." Amun smiled gently. "Please. I do understand how you feel; if it were my sister I would feel the same. But it is not necessary. We are civilized men. We will go inside, we shall talk and have some tea together, and you will see that what we want from you is not so terrible. You will agree to what we ask and your sister will be released unharmed, I promise." He held out his hand again and gestured toward the entryway. "Please," he repeated, and Kemnebi weighed in by placing a heavy palm against the back of Gabriel's neck.

Gabriel stared at Amun for a moment and then turned and walked inside.

SAMMI LOWERED HER BINOCULARS AND CURSED TO herself in French. Suddenly Lucy's kidnapping made sense.

She was standing behind a display of inexpensive jewelry in a shop across from Jumoke's. The shopkeeper, a woman, approached Sammi and asked if she needed assistance.

"No, thank you. Sorry." Sammi left her cover and moved out into the busy lane. She looked for another place where she could stand unnoticed and chose a doorway half hidden in shadow. Keeping one eye on the entrance to Jumoke's, she took out her cell phone and began hastily to type out a message on its miniature keyboard. She had to warn Gabriel, had to explain to him who that man was—

But she didn't get the chance to finish. Before she'd gotten three words into her message, the door she was propped against suddenly opened inward. Sammi stumbled and put out one hand to catch herself—but as she did, a burlap sack was thrown over her head from behind.

"Hey!" she shouted, her voice muffled. She tried to swing an elbow behind her, but her arm was seized in an iron grip. She raised one leg and brought her boot-clad heel down swiftly and heard a grunt of pain. The hold on her arms tightened. She struggled to break free, but there was no way. A moment later, she felt herself lifted off the ground and thrown over someone's shoulder.

The quality of the light filtering through the burlap changed as she was carried inside. She felt the strap of the binoculars snap as it was yanked painfully against her neck. Her cell phone had vanished in the tussle as well. She felt two pairs of hands roughly frisking her, then her own hands were tied behind her back with some sort of narrow cord. She squirmed and fought and shouted till one of the men gave her a chop, hard, through the bag. Her head rang from the blow and she tasted blood—she'd bitten into her cheek. She was lifted again, then carried for a span, and then dumped onto a cold metal surface. She heard what sounded like the doors of a van being slammed shut and locked. The van bounced slightly as someone climbed into the driver's seat, then again when the other man joined him in the passenger's. Sammi resumed shouting and kicked against the side of the van, but if anyone heard there was no sign. The driver started the ignition and drove away.

AMUN LED GABRIEL AND KEMNEBI THROUGH Jumoke's to a storeroom in the back. Heaps of carpets, flat and rolled, lay on the floor. They navigated between them to a small room that served as an office.

Amun took a seat in one of the room's two chairs and gestured for Gabriel to take the other. Kemnebi came around and laid Gabriel's Colt on the table between them.

"How lovely," Amun said, raising the gun and appraising it with a connoisseur's eye. "An antique, isn't it?"

"Yes. And I'm going to want it back."

"Of course. If our talk goes as well as I expect, I will return it to you with pleasure." He set the gun down again and accepted the glass of tea Kemnebi was holding out to him. A scent of mint wafted across the table. Kemnebi held a glass out to Gabriel.

"No, thanks," Gabriel said.

"It's very good," Amun said, "especially when it's so hot outside. No? Well perhaps a bit later." Kemnebi set the glass down in front of Gabriel, some of its contents sloshing out into the saucer.

Amun picked up a cardboard tube from the floor, dug inside it with a finger, and removed a rolled print. He unfurled it, weighing down one corner with Gabriel's gun and another with his saucer. The print showed a black-and-white photograph of a stone tablet covered in hieroglyphics. One corner of the tablet was broken off.

"Do you recognize it, Mister Hunt?" Amun asked.

"Of course," Gabriel said. "Any undergrad would. It's the Rosetta Stone."

"Correct. A relic of ancient Egypt and one of the most important and most valuable artifacts ever discovered. It now unfortunately resides in the British Museum in London."

"So?"

Amun's brown eyes flared. "One day it shall return to Egypt, I promise you that. But that is neither here nor there."

"Well, it's not here," Gabriel said. "It is there."

Amun took a sip of his tea. His hand didn't shake. "I know you are trying to provoke me, Mister Hunt. Perhaps I will do or say something I regret, something you could use to gain an advantage over me." He set the cup down again. "I won't."

"Okay," Gabriel said. "So you won't. What is it you want me to do—break into the British Museum and steal the Rosetta Stone for you?"

"No, no, of course not. Nothing that simple."

"Simple," Gabriel said.

"There's nothing simpler than taking something from a museum," Amun said. "What we want your help with is considerably more difficult."

"You going to tell me, or do I have to keep guessing?"

Amun stretched out a finger and traced it along the edge of the Rosetta Stone. "As you can see, there is a piece missing. Broken off. Lost forever. Who knows what additional information it might have contained, what secrets?"

"What's your point?"

"What if I were to tell you, Mister Hunt, that a second entire tablet exists, twice the size of this missing piece, one that contains even more precious—more powerful—information than the stone in the British Museum? Information that could, quite simply, change the world?"

7

GABRIEL RAISED HIS EYEBROWS.

"I see you are skeptical," Amun said. "What do you know about the Rosetta Stone, Mister Hunt?"

"You want a history lesson, you should ask my brother. He could talk your ear off." Amun said nothing. "It's, what, from the time of Ptolemy—one of the Ptolemys, anyway, something like two hundred B.C., right?"

"That's very good, Mister Hunt," Amun said. "Go on."

"What else. There are three texts on the stone, or more precisely the same text written in three different languages. Comparing them was how Egyptian hieroglyphics were first deciphered." Gabriel remembered Sheba McCoy regaling him with the story in bed one night, tracing the lines of various ancient symbols across his bare chest with a fingertip. He'd always had a thing for linguists, but never more so than that night.

"Go on."

"That's all I've got. As I recall, the text on the stone was nothing too interesting—something about taxes and putting statues in temples, wasn't it?"

"Something like that. It was Ptolemy the Fifth and you were off by four years, but that's better than most Americans could have done. Better than most Egyptians, for that matter. Do you recall how the Stone was found?"

Gabriel had a sudden sense of déjà vu. *The old boy seemed to be turning up everywhere.* "Napoleon's army found it. Around 1800?"

"Seventeen ninety-nine. Bonaparte had led a campaign into Egypt in '98. Having effectively conquered the country, he brought in scientists and archaeologists to rape us of our treasures in the name of 'historical discovery.' The Stone was found in Rashid—an area the French referred to as Rosetta at the time. The history books are sadly incomplete with regard to exactly what happened to the Stone over the next two years, after Napoleon returned to France, leaving his men here to continue their work."

"Didn't the British also invade Egypt around that time?" Gabriel asked.

"Yes. The British *and* the Ottomans. They decided to challenge the French, using my country as a battleground. The French took the Rosetta Stone to Alexandria along with numerous other bits of plunder, in an attempt to keep it all out of their enemies' hands, but it didn't work. The British prevailed, the French surrendered. The French commander, a man named de Menou, tried to keep the Rosetta Stone for himself as personal property. But that ended as you might expect."

"With the Stone in the British Museum."

"Precisely."

"So what about this second tablet?"

Amun poured himself another glass of mint tea. "Are you sure you won't have a drink, Mister Hunt? You know it is an insult to refuse hospitality from an Arab."

"How do I know the tea's not drugged?" Gabriel said.

"You don't," Amun said. "If I wish to drug you, Mister Hunt, you will be drugged. If I wish to kill you, you will be killed. Now drink your tea."

Gabriel lifted the glass to his lips, sniffed, and took a sip.

"You see?" Amun said. "Not everything is a threat, my friend."

"Let's get one thing straight. We're not friends."

Amun shrugged. "Perhaps we will be once you have laid hands on the most important archaeological discovery in the history of the Western world."

"Don't bet on it," Gabriel said.

"Mister Hunt. You can pretend all you like, you will not convince me that you are not curious."

"Sure I'm curious. I'd have been more curious if you hadn't kidnapped my sister."

"Perhaps," Amun said. "But you would have been less likely to turn the Stone over to us rather than to one of your museums once you'd found it."

"How do you even know this second tablet exists? I've never heard about it."

"Yes, well. That is in the nature of secrets: few people hear of them. And this one was kept very secret indeed." Amun raised a hand to stop Gabriel from interrupting. "The Second Stone, as we have come to call it, was a good deal smaller than the first and buried quite a bit deeper in the ground.

Napoleon's brother Louis found it after the main excavation was completed. He unearthed it with the assistance of his private secretary and kept it for the emperor, as a gift. When Louis returned to France in 1799, he brought the Second Stone back with him. But he couldn't restrain himself and described it to his brother in a private letter sent in advance by courier. We have that letter."

"How do you know he was telling the truth about it?" Gabriel said.

"You think he would lie to his brother? To Napoleon Bonaparte? No, no, it was the truth. When he arrived and presented the Second Stone to Napoleon, the Emperor was overjoyed. He spent a week sequestered with the piece and summoned one of his most trusted advisors to his side to examine it with him. We have that letter as well."

"Is that all you've got—a couple of letters? I mean, they might fetch a good price at Christie's, but…"

"That is not all we have," Amun said. "We have been searching for the Second Stone for well over thirty years, Mister Hunt. We have chased down false leads by the dozen, we have questioned people who we thought might be harboring information about its whereabouts, and one halting, painful step at a time, we have drawn closer to its hiding place. And we believe we have now found it."

"So why don't you go get it, if you know where it is?"

"We know *generally* where it is," Amun said, "not precisely. And we also know that the location is protected, both mechanically and by a secret society sworn to keep the Second Stone ever from coming to light again."

"What do you mean, 'mechanically'?"

"When Napoleon finished his examination of the Second Stone, he ordered the aide he had summoned—an engineer of some repute—to take the Stone to Napoleon's birthplace in Corsica and hide it there, in a cave near Ajaccio. Napoleon worked closely with this engineer to design the hiding place. We believe the vault in which the Second Stone was placed contains a number of traps—deadly ones, Mister Hunt, based on Napoleon's own ideas. To prevent the Stone from being found or stolen, you understand."

"And the secret society?"

"That was Louis' doing. He organized the group to keep watch over the Stone's location. This small group of Corsicans has passed the knowledge down, father to son, through ten generations. They still exist today."

"And how do you know that? Another letter?"

"No, Mister Hunt," Amun said. "Much simpler than that. We succeeded in capturing one of them. He told us much before he died."

"But not the location of the cave."

"Not its precise location, no. He would have, eventually. But he was too weak. His heart…" Amun made a gesture with one hand, a closed fist opening.

A second Rosetta Stone. Gabriel was having some trouble wrapping his brain around the idea. It would be a treasure, to be sure—a priceless one that men might die to possess. But why would they die to keep its mere existence a secret?

"What's so special about this Second Stone? There's got to be something more to it than its archeological significance."

Amun smiled. He leaned forward across the table. "After seeing what was inscribed on the Second Stone, Napoleon Bonaparte conquered Europe. He was a strong soldier before—but after, for a time…? He was unstoppable. He was a god."

GABRIEL PUT BOTH HANDS ON THE ARMS OF HIS chair, started to stand. Kemnebi stepped closer.

"What is it, Mister Hunt?" Amun said. "We are not done."

"Oh, yes we are," Gabriel said. "I'm not searching for some magic stone you think will give you the power to conquer the world."

"Don't be rash," Amun said. "Your sister will die if you walk out of here now. And so will you."

"For heaven's sake," Gabriel said. "How good a magic stone could it have been? Napoleon lost!"

"Sit down!" Amun snatched up Gabriel's Colt and pulled back the hammer. "Or would you rather be shot with your own gun?"

Gabriel sat.

"First of all, Mister Hunt, I did not say it was a *magic* stone. I only said it was contemporaneous with the Rosetta Stone and contained an inscription of sufficient interest that Napoleon spent a week examining it."

"Examining what?" Gabriel said, exasperated. "He couldn't have read it—the Rosetta Stone itself wasn't even translated for twenty more years!"

"Be that as it may. He inspected it, and somehow emerged changed. Transformed. By all accounts, it was the inscription on the Second Stone that gave him the power to achieve what he did. You may call it magic if you wish; I prefer to think of it as the will of the old gods, those who gave the pharaohs their power. Bonaparte gained power he should never have had. He gained… I am not sure what to call it. Charisma.

The mantle of a great leader. Whatever along these lines he had before was multiplied a hundredfold. A thousandfold. He became the Napoleon of history books, the famed emperor of Europe. He was a changed man."

"Who *lost!*"

"Yes, ultimately. He made some serious mistakes and was brought down—but he came closer to dominating the world than anyone since Alexander or Genghis Khan."

"Did they have magic stones too?"

"Who knows? Perhaps. All we care about is what Bonaparte had." Amun took another swallow of his tea. His hand was shaking now, very slightly, and Gabriel saw sweat dotting his brow. The man was not completely unflappable. "He had no right to it," Amun said. "It was ours—it was Egypt's. The stone and the power it conveyed. And you are going to help us get it back."

Gabriel stood once more. Kemnebi leaned toward him, grinding the knuckles of one enormous hand against the palm of the other.

"I'm not leaving," Gabriel said. "Just need the bathroom. Too much tea."

Amun nodded at Kemnebi. "Show him where it is."

The big man extended one long arm, pointing. He followed close behind as Gabriel walked between two tall piles of rugs. A wooden door stood open and through it Gabriel could see a small cubicle with a sink and commode.

He shut the door behind him, unbuckled his belt, and went through the motions of using the facility, trusting the sound to travel through the thin door. Meanwhile, he reached into his jacket pocket and dug out his cell phone. He saw a text message from Sammi on the screen:

THAT'S THE PRO

That was all there was. Just the three words, and the third possibly not even complete. *That's the problem…? That's the professional…?* What had she meant to type—and what had prevented her from finishing the message?

Pressing the phone's tiny loudspeaker tightly against his ear to muffle its sound, Gabriel thumbed the icon to dial Sammi's cell phone. It rang just once and then went to voicemail.

Damn.

After zipping his pants and washing his hands, Gabriel swung the door open.

Kemnebi and Amun were standing there, waiting for him. Before Gabriel could say a word, Kemnebi grabbed him roughly by the shoulders and slammed him against the wall. The big man patted him down until he felt the phone through Gabriel's jacket. He groped inside and held it aloft like a prize.

"You should have known better," Amun said. "We can't allow you to be in contact with the outside world, Mister Hunt."

Kemnebi dropped the phone on the floor and then stomped on it with his boot, smashing the thirty-thousand dollar device to pieces.

"Oh, and you can forget about your female companion," Amun added. "By now, I am afraid she is no longer among the living."

8

IT WAS DIFFICULT FOR SAMMI TO TELL HOW FAST THE van was going. From the smoothness of the drive, she suspected they were on an expressway.

She'd given up yelling and kicking when it became clear it was doing no good. Instead, she concentrated on the ropes around her wrists. When she had been her father's assistant, she had used thicker cords that were easier to manipulate. These felt as narrow as shoelaces; they were tight and dug painfully into her skin.

The secret of slipping rope ties was to prepare for the escape prior to being bound. Houdini would stand in poses that expanded his muscles so that when he relaxed his pose after being tied he gained the millimeters of slack he needed. Another approach was to discreetly influence the person doing the binding into tying his knots a specific way—like using a magician's "force" to compel the choice of a particular playing card. Or you could use your fingers and wrists to twist the knot as it was being secured—the so-called Kellar method, which Sammi's father had taught her. Unfortunately, she hadn't had the opportunity to do any of these things.

The van hit a bump and Sammi stifled a yelp. The floor was unpadded corrugated metal and any time they passed over an uneven spot in the pavement she slammed against it. With her arms trussed tightly behind her and her shoulders aching from the strain, getting banged around like this was no pleasure.

She continued to work on the ropes as the terrain changed. She felt the vehicle slow and the road become rougher.

With an effort that almost made her pass out, she managed to force one of the constricting ropes up over the fleshy tissue of her right palm, the thickest part of her hand. The thin cord tore into her skin as she worked her wrists and palms back and forth, loosening the bonds a tiny fraction at a time.

A few minutes later the sounds outside the van changed. Sammi could no longer hear other traffic. The vehicle was not only traveling on a rougher road—it was traveling on an empty one.

Not a good sign.

She sped up her efforts, using a fingernail to saw at the rope, struggling to apply pressure with her index finger.

Then her nail broke.

Sammi cursed aloud but kept sawing. It hurt like hell—but maybe the ragged edge of the broken nail would get through the rope that much quicker.

The van made a sharp left turn that threw her against the inside wall, then it continued on over a rocky, bumpy road. She tried to maintain her concentration.

Pretend it's an underwater trunk escape. You're being buffeted by the current, you've got 90 seconds of air, you've got to get out.

Now.

With an excruciating effort, she slipped two fingers beneath the rope and strained to squeeze through the narrow opening she'd managed to create. The sweat on her palms provided some lubrication, but—was it enough?

Just a little more. She could feel it. She was almost there.

Which was a good thing, since the van was slowing further.

Finally… the rope slipped. She pulled her fingers through and felt the rope slide free onto the floor of the van. The next thing was the burlap bag. With trembling fingers, she untied the cord securing it around her neck and stripped it off. She drew in a deep breath—the air in the back of a filthy van had never tasted so fresh. She took a moment to get her bearings.

A metal partition separated the van's cab from the back. There was nothing else back here with her.

Now what?

She didn't have a plan. She didn't have a weapon. She had only one advantage—she wasn't tied up anymore, and they didn't know it.

Moments later the van pulled to a stop. She crawled over to the back doors as she heard the men get out of the cab. Then footsteps on gravel, moving to the rear.

Keys rattled in the lock. They were about to open the doors.

Sammi positioned herself on her back, her feet against the doors.

They started to swing open.

Sammi kicked out, hard, hitting both men, one

heavy metal door in each kidnapper's face. She lurched to her feet and jumped out of the van. One of the men, a short, stocky Egyptian in khakis and hiking boots, was on his side on the ground, groping at a shoulder holster. The other, a taller man with hair the color of cold ash and cheeks pocked with acne scars, was still on his feet. She kneed him in the groin as hard as she could. The man howled and dropped to his knees. She gave him another knee, this time to the jaw, and he went down.

The other man, meanwhile, had managed to get his gun out. Sammi fell face first in the dirt and heard a bullet speed by overhead, ricocheting off the side of the van. She reached over to the unconscious man beside her and, with a heave, dragged his body between her and the shooter. He fired again, but high, trying not to hit his fallen comrade.

The comrade had a holster as well, on his hip, and Sammi wasted no time in snatching the pistol out of it. She was no expert with guns, but she knew enough to take the safety off and aim it in the right direction.

The man across from her leveled his gun right back at her. He called something to her in Arabic, the tone condescending. *Put down the gun,* she imagined, or maybe, *You're not going to pull that trigger, are you, little lady?*

She pulled the trigger.

The look of surprise that blossomed on the man's face was matched only by the sudden spread of a red bloom across the front of his shirt, like a time-lapse movie of a rose opening.

He fell backwards, blood pooling beneath him.

Sammi scrambled to her feet and glanced around. It was a desolate patch of land, home to what looked like an abandoned rock quarry or possibly a one-time archaeological dig. A deep, narrow trench had been dug in the ground.

They had planned to kill her and bury her here.

She thought briefly about filling the grave with the body of the man she'd shot, but there was no telling how soon the other one would come to. She could have shot him as well—she considered this briefly—but she decided that one shooting in a day, and that in self-defense, was her limit. She was not a squeamish woman, but she drew the line at shooting an unconscious man.

She did hold onto his gun, though.

Returning to the van, she climbed in behind the wheel, found the keys in the ignition. Her purse and cell phone were in the well between the seats, along with the binoculars with the broken strap.

Sammi closed the door and started the engine. She could see Cairo's skyline in the distance. Gabriel was somewhere back there. She floored the gas.

9

AMUN LED GABRIEL THROUGH AN ARCHWAY AND
into a modestly appointed dining room. A table had
been set for two.

Kemnebi followed close behind.

"I thought you might like a bite before we embark
on our journey," Amun announced as he gestured to a
chair. "Please."

"I'm not hungry," Gabriel answered. "I had lunch."

"Come, come. We have already discussed the insult
of refusing hospitality. Try some of our delicacies. I
don't expect you to clean your plate."

Gabriel took one of the seats. Amun bowed slightly
and then sat across from him. Kemnebi stood near
another archway that was draped with long, hanging
curtains. He clapped his hands. A young woman
wearing a *niqab* entered with a tray. The pungent
aromas of cooked food wafted into the dining room.

She placed a basket of pita bread on the table and

poured two glasses of water. Along with a pair of steaming bowls, Gabriel noted the several sets of utensils on her tray. Including knives.

The woman put the bowls of greenish soup in front of both men and doled out a spoon apiece from the stack of cutlery, then carried the tray out of reach, standing with it against one of the walls.

"Have you tried our molokhiyya soup?" Amun asked. "It's made from a vegetable that's distinctly Egyptian." He took a piece of pita with his right hand and dunked it into his bowl. Gabriel did the same. The soup was salty but very good.

"You've been to Egypt before, I take it?"

"Many times," Gabriel replied. "Never had the soup, though."

"I am pleased," Amun said, "to introduce a man as worldly as you to a new experience."

"I've never had my sister kidnapped either," Gabriel said.

"Or your traveling companion killed, I imagine."

"No," Gabriel said, "that one I've had."

"Well, I'm sorry to burden you with it again. With either of these distasteful events. Rest assured it gives me no pleasure to do these things. I am not a sadist, Mister Hunt. Merely a man with a purpose."

"So was Torquemada," Gabriel said.

"Yes, yes, Torquemada," Amun said. "Eat your soup."

Gabriel took another spoonful, trying hard to control his temper. It was difficult to converse politely with the man responsible for Lucy's kidnapping and Sammi's present situation. Whatever that might be. He knew how skilled she was at getting out of impossible traps; he wouldn't believe she was dead till he got some proof.

"What exactly did you do to my... traveling companion?"

"Miss Ficatier?" Amun said. "You were told to come alone to our rendezvous. Let's leave it at that."

"If she's been harmed—"

"What? What, Mister Hunt? You are in no position to make threats. If I were you, I'd resign myself to cooperating. After all, I am sure your sister means more to you than some woman you just met in Nice."

"She's my sister's friend."

"She should have stayed home." Amun snapped his fingers and the woman with the tray came forward again and collected their bowls. She vanished for a moment through the curtains, then returned with something new on the tray, a platter of rice topped with chunks of cooked lamb and onion. The dish smelled of marjoram and lemon juice. Once again, Gabriel eyed the utensils.

"May I have a fork?" Gabriel asked.

"It is customary to use your bread," Amun said. He demonstrated by scooping up some of the food with a piece of pita.

The woman was refilling their water glasses. As she turned back toward the kitchen, Gabriel shifted his foot to catch the hem of her garment, a full-body *burqa*. She took two steps before the tug on the fabric trapped under Gabriel's heel overbalanced her and she tripped, sending the tray and extra utensils flying.

Gabriel jumped up from the table to help her. "Are you all right?"

Her veil—the *niqab*—had slipped to one side, revealing her features. Embarrassed, she pulled it back into place.

He put a hand on her arm to help her up, but she jerked it out of his grasp. He gathered up the scattered utensils instead and put them back on the tray. "I'm sorry," he whispered, in Arabic, as he handed the tray to her; it was one of the few expressions he knew. Behind the veil, he could only see her eyes as they glanced at the pile of knives and forks and then back at him. There was a question in her gaze. Gabriel shook his head minutely. She turned away and vanished through the curtains.

"I apologize, Mister Hunt, for Nabirye's clumsiness," Amun said. "She will be disciplined."

"Don't do that, it was my fault. I stepped on her dress by accident."

"You are kind to try to protect her, but I know you are lying," Amun said.

"I'm not—I did step on her dress—"

"Yes," Amun said. "But not by accident. Kemnebi, please search Mister Hunt's sleeves."

Reluctantly, Gabriel submitted to his third pat-down of the day. Kemnebi found the long-handled dinner knife he'd shot up his right sleeve in the confusion. The big man brandished it in Gabriel's face, tweaking the underside of his chin with the point.

"How many times do I have to tell you," Amun said, "that you won't be able to put anything over on me? It is getting tiresome."

"All right," Gabriel said, sitting at the table again. "Consider the lesson learned."

He scooted his chair closer to the table, his trouser leg neatly covering the second knife he'd grabbed. The blade was snug against his calf, the handle held in place by the elastic of his sock.

Gabriel scooped some rice onto his piece of pita and

stuck it into his mouth.

"When we have finished," Amun said, "Kemnebi will take us to the airport. We're going to take a short plane ride."

"Where to?"

"Morocco."

"If you wanted me in Morocco, why didn't you just have me meet you there in the first place?"

"I had business to attend to here in Cairo. Besides, I had to make sure that anyone you brought with you for protection could be disposed of. As we have seen, I was right to be concerned."

"And what's in Morocco?"

"Oh, many things are in Morocco," Amun said. He ate another mouthful of the meat. "If you are well behaved, Mister Hunt, perhaps we shall let you see your sister."

Gabriel didn't say anything.

"We shall spend the night in Marrakesh. The following day we leave for Corsica. In between, we will provide you with access to all the materials we have in our possession on the subject of the Second Stone. We want you to be well prepared when you go after it."

Gabriel thought about the task they were proposing—if you could call insistence at gunpoint "proposing." Was it really possible that there was a second Rosetta Stone, one that somehow held the secret to Napoleon's world-dominating reign? Gabriel had learned long ago never to dismiss anything as impossible. He'd seen things in his travels that no sane man would believe if he hadn't witnessed them himself. And yet… the thought of a mystical inscription from the time of the pharaohs that somehow gave the French Emperor the ability to conquer millions? It was a lot to accept.

On the other hand, even if the legend of the inscription was just that—a legend—the stone itself might well be real. And the traps protecting it.

"How much do you know about the Stone's hiding place? This vault you say Napoleon designed."

Amun looked up from his plate. "Not as much as we would like. But everything we do know, you will learn in the next twenty-four hours. We would prefer if you didn't die in the attempt, Mister Hunt."

"That makes two of us," Gabriel said.

Amun waved at his nearly empty plate and at Gabriel's nearly full one. "If you are finished…?" Gabriel nodded, pushed his plate away from him. "Very well. Then we shall depart."

SAMMI RACED BACK TO THE KHAN EL-KHALILI, PARKED the van down the street from Jumoke's, and attempted to call Gabriel again. His phone wasn't even ringing, just going directly to voicemail; there was definitely something wrong. She was tempted to walk into the carpet shop and see if she could turn up any sign of him, but she knew that would be a mistake. Free, she might be of some help; captured, she'd be useless.

The two-hour time limit had long since passed, so the smart thing would be simply to call Michael Hunt. It's what Gabriel had instructed her to do. But Michael was in New York, five thousand miles away. What could he do for them?

Before she could decide on an alternative plan, a black limousine rolled up through the mass of people in the street and stopped in front of Jumoke's. As Sammi watched, Gabriel appeared in the shop's entryway.

He was followed by the same two men who'd led him inside earlier. The three of them came out of the shop and headed straight for the limo. Gabriel looked unharmed, at least. The big man opened the back door and held it while the others climbed in. Then he climbed in after them. The driver leaned on the horn to scatter the pedestrians that had gathered around the car, then pulled away and drove slowly down the street.

Sammi started the van and followed.

The limo made its way out of the bazaar and onto Al-Azhar. Sammi stayed back several car lengths—the van belonged to the Alliance, after all, and she didn't want them to spot and recognize it trailing them. Fortunately, it was difficult to lose a black stretch limo on the streets of Cairo.

They made several turns until the limo reached the expressway leading south out of the city. Sammi followed them onto the ramp and picked up speed but kept a steady distance behind them. It wasn't long until the skyscrapers gave way to low-rises and the urban sprawl grew thinner. Eventually the limo exited the expressway and drove along a stretch of road to an airfield surrounded by a barbed-wired fence. Sammi stopped at the edge of the fence. Through the binoculars she watched the limo pull up to the gated entrance. A sign on the fence warned in Arabic and English, *PRIVATE! NO TRESPASSING!*, and a security camera watched anyone who drove up. After a moment the gate lifted and the limo rolled in. The driver parked just a few yards past the fence, in a small lot next to the control tower. Sammi watched the men get out of the car and go inside the building. She scanned the rest of the property. Beside the tower was a single hangar; a small twin-engine corporate jet sat on the only runway. It appeared to be ready to go—its hatch was open and a staircase attached to the fuselage led down to the tarmac.

Sure enough, it wasn't three minutes before Gabriel and the other two emerged from the tower, together with a pair of men in flight uniforms. They walked toward the jet and climbed aboard. The staircase automatically withdrew into the fuselage and the hatch closed. Moments later the plane was in the air.

Now what?

Sammi took a deep breath, let it out slowly. She checked in the rear-view mirror to make sure her hair was all tucked under the headscarf again, and drove up to the gate. When you didn't want to be noticed, she'd learned, the best way was sometimes to just walk boldly through the front door. The key was to look like you belonged, like there was no reason to pay attention to you. In this case, the fact that the van she was driving was one of theirs should help—as long as they didn't take too close a look at her.

She waited, stared straight ahead, and tried not to look directly into the security camera. After a moment she honked the van's horn.

Come on…!

She heard a click beside her and slowly the gate began to rise. With her heart racing, she drove inside and parked next to the tower. She slipped the handgun into her purse and got out. Past a pair of glass doors, she saw a reception desk, unmanned, and a flight of stairs. She climbed them two at a time.

At the top of the stairs was the control room. One man sat in front of a bank of monitors, watching radar sweeps in glowing green. His eyes widened at the sight of her and he reached for a telephone.

"Don't move!" Sammi shouted, pointing the gun at him.

The man cautiously raised his hands.

"The plane that just left, where was it going?"

He shook his head.

She pointed the gun at the ceiling and pulled the trigger. The acoustic tiles splintered into shrapnel and rained down on the man and his monitors. He flinched.

"Answer me!"

"M-M-Marrakesh…"

She approached him, the gun extended before her.

"Please… don't shoot me…"

"I'll only shoot you if you make me," Sammi said.

"Now: what other planes do you have at this airstrip that can make it to Marrakesh?"

"None," the man said. "That was the only plane here."

She'd had a bad feeling he was going to say that. Without lowering the gun, she dug her cell phone out of her purse and jabbed at the screen with her thumb.

"Hello?" The voice on the other end of the phone was reedy and nasal.

"Michael Hunt?"

"Yes? Who is this?"

"I'm a friend of your sister's. And your brother's. They're both in trouble and I'm trying to help them."

"What? Who are you? Where are you calling from? What's the—"

"I'll answer all your questions later," Sammi said. "But right now I need you to get me on a plane to Marrakesh."

10

THE HAWKER 400 LANDED AT ANOTHER PRIVATE airstrip near the foothills of Morocco's Atlas Mountains. The sun cast an orange glow over a landscape that was already reddish to begin with; it wasn't for nothing that Marrakesh was known as the Red City.

Back in his misspent youth, Marrakesh had been one of Gabriel's favorite places in Africa. It was too bad that his first time back in years had to be under such undesirable circumstances.

As he was escorted down the steps to the tarmac, Gabriel felt the knife still pressing against his calf. It had been a gamble, not attempting to use it in the limo—a gamble that they'd be taking him to a private runway rather than a commercial airport with metal detectors. But he figured they had weapons of their own they wouldn't want detected; if nothing else, Kemnebi was still carrying Gabriel's Colt. And the prospect of a fight in the back of a moving car against two men bigger than he was had not greatly appealed. Besides, if Lucy was in Marrakesh, Marrakesh was where he needed to be.

Another limousine, this one blindingly white, waited at the foot of the steps. Gabriel was ushered inside. He saw two men already there, seated on the long padded bench behind the driver's seat.

One of them, a thin man sporting a tidy pencil mustache, extended a hand. Gabriel ignored it. "Have you been to Marrakesh before, Mister Hunt?"

"Once or twice."

The limo pulled out of the airfield and onto a highway.

"It is a beautiful city," the man said. "Not like Cairo, of course. But it has many pleasures."

Gabriel merely stared, and the man, having run out of small talk for the moment, fell silent.

After half an hour they came to the famed Djemaa el Fna, the central square in the medina. It was the largest of its type in Africa. Gabriel saw the traditional water sellers, the snake charmers, the acrobats and jugglers performing for the hordes of tourists who were gathered about, snapping pictures. He saw a group of Chleuh dancing boys and beside them an old man leading a troupe of trained Barbary apes through a comic routine. And then there were the peddlers, of course, vendors of everything from souvenirs to dubious medicines, and the food stalls offering every sort of edible. The smells drifted into the limousine through the air vents, as did the muffled sounds of traditional Berber music and the clamor of the crowd.

The driver circled the square and went down a relatively empty side street. They stopped a block away and parked near what appeared to be an abandoned building made of sandstone and stucco. It was four stories tall, and the windows and front door were boarded up. Signs in Arabic looked to Gabriel like warnings to trespassers to keep out.

Gabriel got out of the car with the other men. Amun pointed back toward the Djemaa el Fna. "This way."

"We're going to buy souvenirs?" Gabriel asked. "I could use a pit viper or two."

They walked the block back, entered the square, and moved to the right along the perimeter. Gabriel knew that if he was going to make a break for it, now was the time to do it. He could easily lose himself in the crowd, or at least cause enough of a diversion to get away. But that wouldn't help Lucy. In fact, it might put her in greater danger. So he kept walking.

Kemnebi led the way around a wooden cabin with a striped fabric roof; under the fabric a fat man worked the lever of an ancient orange reamer, spilling an endless stream of juice into cups, which a boy who looked like his son sold to a line of thirsty tourists. Next to the cabin, a water seller insistently argued for the superiority of his beverage, shouting in thickly accented English, "Juice make you *more* thirsty! Clean water!" Looking at the man's swollen leather pouch and the clattering tin cups he made his customers use, Gabriel questioned the truth of his claims. Even if the water was clean when it went *into* the cup…

Amun took Gabriel's arm and steered him toward a carpet shop. It looked more or less identical to Jumoke's, except that the sign over the entryway here said *Nizan*.

Kemnebi strode up to a closed wooden door in the side of the building and rapped on it. After a moment, a man opened it and greeted first Kemnebi and then

Amun in Arabic. This was Nizan, presumably; he might have been Jumoke's brother.

Amun and Kemnebi followed Nizan into the shop through the side door, Gabriel trailing behind them, and the two other men from the limousine coming after him. Nizan lifted a curtain and led them all into a back room. He then squatted, lifted the corner of a carpet on the floor, and revealed a hinged trap door with a metal ring in the center. The ring was secured with a hasp and a heavy padlock. Nizan fished a key out of his vest pocket and used it to remove the lock. He put both hands inside the ring and grunted as he lifted it. The door creaked open, revealing a staircase leading down.

Kemnebi was the first to descend, then Amun prodded Gabriel to follow. The underground passageway he found himself in at the foot of the stairs was long and curving, but well lit by bulbs dangling overhead. Gabriel thought the tunnel itself looked old, despite the presence of electric lights; it might have been carved centuries ago, the markings on the stone suggesting blows from hand tools rather than any sort of heavy machinery. He wondered what its original purpose had been. Something unsavory, he was sure.

They walked for what felt like about a city block and before coming to another staircase leading back up. Kemnebi pressed a button on an intercom box mounted on the wall. They heard a scuffling of feet above, then another trap door opened and the group ascended, single file.

They emerged into a small room lined with shelves of food supplies—it looked like the pantry of a modern home, Gabriel thought. Two men stood waiting for them, guns in hand. They greeted Amun and Kemnebi warmly but regarded Gabriel with suspicion.

The trap door was lowered and a carpet replaced over it. The men walked them into a living room furnished with a combination of modern and traditional Arabic fittings. In one corner, a large whiteboard stood, covered with scrawled diagrams and words Gabriel couldn't read. There were curtains drawn over all the windows. Through the curtains Gabriel could see that the windows were boarded up from the outside.

"We're back where we started," Gabriel said. "We just made a big circle."

"That is correct, Mister Hunt," Amun said.

"Why?"

"I am sure you can appreciate that we prefer to keep our activities out of view of prying eyes," Amun said. "The way we came is the only way in."

"I guess I'm supposed to feel fortunate that you're letting me see the place," Gabriel said.

"You should, Mister Hunt. You are the first non-Egyptian who has."

"What about my sister?"

Amun smiled thinly. "She was blindfolded, of course."

"And why do I get this special treatment?"

"Because you work for us now," Amun said. "We must begin trusting each other sometime."

"Can I ask you something? If your *raison d'être*—pardon my French—is resurrecting the glory of Egypt, why didn't you set up this secret clubhouse there?"

"We have found," Amun said, "that it is best to operate outside of Egypt. There are certain groups within our country—the government, for one—that support what we do in theory but cannot publicly condone some of the more... decisive acts the Alliance has carried out."

"You mean like torture, kidnapping, and theft?"

"Yes," Amun said. "Those would be examples. Of course what we do is simply retribution for crimes committed against Egypt, and many in the government have told us privately that they wholeheartedly support our actions. But to say so publicly would be impossible."

"I can't imagine why," Gabriel said drily.

"Your media would leap upon it instantly," Amun said, "the international media would follow, and any politician who expressed solidarity with us would be hounded from office by the chorus of outraged voices. The media, after all, are in the control of the Jews, who would like nothing more than to see—"

"Yes, yes, the Jews," Gabriel said. "Eat your soup."

Amun fell silent, but the look in his eyes was vicious. Finally he spoke. "We need not like one another, Mister Hunt. But we do have to work together. I suggest you show me a bit more respect."

"Actually, Amun, I think you have it backwards. I think you need me. And I think you know you need me. You've been looking for your Second Stone for thirty years and you haven't found it yet. You think I can get it for you. Fine—maybe I can. But if you want me to cooperate, you're going to have to show me and my sister a bit more respect."

"We have shown your sister enormous respect," Amun said. "We have not killed her."

"Well, that's a start," Gabriel said. "But we're going to need more than that."

"For instance?"

"You can let me see her. I'd also like my gun back."

"You will see your sister in an hour. Your gun is

another story. You will get it back when I am certain
you will not use it to harm me or anyone else here."
Amun gestured to the men who had let them in, who
were now standing on either side of Gabriel. They took
hold of his arms. "Now. I *respectfully* ask that you join
me in my study so that you might learn about the work
you have ahead of you."

The two men forcefully propelled Gabriel forward,
practically lifting him by the elbows. Together, they
climbed the stairs to the second floor. The men shoved
him into a dark room lined with bookshelves and took
up positions on either side of the doorway. Amun
seated himself on the edge of a desk made of some
highly polished dark wood, almost black. A map on
the wall behind him showed the geography of Corsica
in enormous detail. There were pushpins stuck into it
in various locations.

Amun spoke curtly in Arabic to one of the men
by the door, then turned to Gabriel. "Would you like
something to eat or drink? You have a lot of reading
ahead of you."

"I could use a bourbon and ice."

Amun shot him a look. "No alcohol in a Muslim
house, Mister Hunt."

"Water, then," Gabriel said. "Just not from that guy
out in the square, please."

Amun communicated the request to the guard and
the man ran off.

"Why don't we start with this map, Mister Hunt."

Gabriel came closer and studied it. Most of the pins
were clustered in the lower half of the island, close to
the capital city of Ajaccio and a little further south,
near the towns of Filitosa, Propriano, and Sartene.

"I've been there," Gabriel said. "That region's where

all the prehistoric sites were discovered."

"Correct. Fascinating places, old as Stonehenge. Full of caves and houses made of rocks and strange menhirs arranged in circles."

"You think the Second Stone is hidden somewhere around there?"

"We know it is. In one of these prehistoric forests close to Ajaccio." Amun pointed to a bulging leather folder on the desk. "Inside here you will find copies of all the documents I mentioned earlier. Some in Italian, some in French; one or two in very bad English. I can translate the ones—"

"Not necessary," Gabriel said. "I should be fine."

"There is also a good deal of material about Napoleon in the folder." Amun opened it and thumbed through a stack of stapled documents, some yellow with age, some gray and faded almost to illegibility. The stack was as thick the manuscript of a book, and not a skinny paperback, either. Gabriel estimated there were five or six hundred pages.

The guard returned carrying a cup of coffee, a bottle of water and a glass. Amun took the coffee; Gabriel took the rest.

"I'm going to leave you alone for a while, Mister Hunt," Amun said. He looked over at an ornate, golden clock on one of the shelves. "Maybe a bit more than an hour. Please look over all the materials, and feel free to take down any of the books you're curious about. Do not try to escape. Odji and Ubaid will stay here with you, and Kemnebi is right outside the door. He'll come and fetch you when your sister is ready to receive you."

"What do you mean, ready? Why wouldn't she be ready now?"

"She's not awake yet," Amun said. "It takes some time for the drug to exit her system."

Amun left the room and shut the door. Gabriel heard the click of the lock. It hardly mattered; maybe Sammi could have found a way out of this place, but he didn't see one. There were no windows in the room, only shelves of books, and the two guards inside could see his every move. Plus there was the giant of a man outside the door, and the three other men in the building, all of them hostile. And no way in or out of the building other than a narrow tunnel...

He sighed and settled into the chair behind the desk. The document on the top of the stack showed a sketch of the Second Stone, supposedly drawn by the private secretary who'd dug it up at Louis' direction; the drawing showed the stone still half buried in the desert sand, a skeletal arm and skull beside it, a retinue of soldiers on horses milling about in the background in native garb. Gabriel turned the page. The next document was a map of Corsica, similar to the one on the wall, with markings where the pushpins were. A single word of Arabic had been written on the map next to a cluster of markings and underlined heavily. Gabriel copied it onto a scrap of paper and stuck it in his pocket.

Then on to the first long text document, an account from the nineteenth century describing how the Second Stone had been transported from France to Corsica. The language of the document was dense and old-fashioned, and Gabriel felt a headache coming on before he'd made it through the first page. But he had an hour to kill—maybe more—and he might as well use it productively. He rested his chin on his hand and kept reading.

* * *

NINETY MINUTES LATER, THE LOCK CLICKED AGAIN,
the door swung open, and Kemnebi stepped inside.
He said just one word—the first, Gabriel realized, he'd
ever heard the big man speak.

"Come."

Gabriel stood, allowed himself to be steered out
into the hallway and up another flight of stairs. They
approached a closed door with a guard stationed in
front of it, a man with a sullen look, several gold teeth
glinting dully in his mouth, and four raw scratches
raking diagonally across his left cheek. The guard
stepped aside and Kemnebi knocked.

A tired-sounding voice answered from inside: "Yes?
What do you want?"

It was Lucy's voice. Gabriel felt his heart race. He
hadn't seen her since the night she'd shown up in the
townhouse on Sutton Place, begging him to help get
a friend of hers out of jail. He'd done what Lucy had
asked, but it hadn't quite turned out the way either of
them had intended, and he hadn't heard from her in
the six months since.

Kemnebi held out his hand. The guard passed him
a set of keys. Kemnebi picked one out and unlocked
the door.

"Fifteen minutes," he said to Gabriel in the low
rumble he had for a voice, and then he pushed the
door open.

11

"GABRIEL!"

"Hey!" He caught his sister in his arms as she rushed unsteadily forward.

Kemnebi shut the door behind them and locked it from the outside.

Lucy was shivering although it wasn't at all cold in the room. She seemed thinner even than the time he'd seen her in Istanbul—their first meeting after nine years apart—and she'd been awfully thin then. Gabriel took hold of her arms and stepped back to look at her.

She was dressed in blue jeans and a black T-shirt with a peeling image of the Eiffel Tower on it in white. Her short-cropped hair had recently been dyed, dark green down to the roots. A tattoo of entwined serpents poked out from under one of the T-shirt's short sleeves, one of a prowling jaguar from under the other. There was a piercing in her left eyebrow that Gabriel hadn't noticed six months earlier.

"Are you all right?"

"Yeah. I'm okay."

"You look like you've lost weight."

"You try being kidnapped sometime. Best diet in the world."

Gabriel looked around the room. It looked more like a bedroom than like a cell, complete with a desk, a chest of drawers, a bookshelf full of books and magazines, a small television set. An open door led to a bathroom with a shower. There was even a window—though like the ones downstairs it was securely boarded up, and it looked like they'd installed metal bars across it outside the glass for good measure. Which made it a cell no matter how nice the furnishings might be.

"I'm going to get you out of here, Lucy."

"Cifer," she said, quietly but firmly.

He put one hand along the side of her face, felt a muscle in her cheek tremble. "Did they hurt you?"

She shook her head. "Not too bad. I got a bit banged up when they broke into my apartment—but so did they. And I haven't exactly been a shrinking wallflower since. It's why they keep drugging me. You saw Chigaru out there in the hall?"

"The guy with the scratches on his face?"

"Guess who gave 'em to him?" She held up her right hand and made a clawing motion through the air. She swayed a bit as she did so, though, and Gabriel led her over to the bed, sat her down. He pulled out a chair and sat beside her.

"Chigaru," she said. "He told me it means 'hound.' His parents knew what they were doing when they named him."

"Why?" Gabriel said. "What did he do to you?"

"Less than he wanted to," Lucy said.

Gabriel found his fists clenching involuntarily.

"It's okay, Gabriel," Lucy said, patting him on one fist. "I can take care of myself. Hell, I figured maybe he'd be my ticket out of here. I've slept with worse-looking guys for less."

"There are some things an older brother doesn't need to know," Gabriel muttered, standing up again, pacing.

"How'd you find me?" Lucy asked.

"They found me," Gabriel said. "Sent a note to Michael saying my helping them was the price for letting you go."

"Helping them do what?"

"Find something they're looking for," Gabriel said. "A stone—an artifact from ancient Egypt that they say is hidden in Corsica."

"Why Corsica?"

"It's a long story," Gabriel said.

Lucy stared at him, concerned. "Are you going to do it?"

"I'm going to do what it takes to get you out of here."

"Do you really think they'll let me go if you get this thing for them? That they'll let *you* go…?"

Gabriel shook his head. "But they aren't going to hurt either of us as long as they still need me to get it. That gives us an advantage."

"A small one," she said.

"Yeah," Gabriel said, but he grinned and chucked her gently under the chin. "But how much of one do I need?"

He saw her eyes warm to the prospect of a rescue. She'd always believed in him—more than she should have, maybe. But a bit of confidence wasn't a bad thing, a bit of hope. She needed something to restore her strength.

Some food would help. He went to the door and pounded on it with the side of his fist.

"What are you doing?" she said.

"Getting you some food."

The lock turned and the door opened. It was Chigaru.

"Hey," Gabriel said, his voice low. "I want you to bring her some food. Right now. And—hold on." Chigaru had started to turn away, but Gabriel snagged the front of his shirt in his fist, turned him around. Chiagru looked down at the bunched fabric angrily. "I want you to know something else. If you touch my sister again, I'll kill you. Do we understand each other?"

"Take your hand off me," Chigaru said.

"Do we understand each other?"

The look in Gabriel's eyes was impossible not to understand. Gabriel let go of Chigaru's shirt, smoothed down the creased fabric. "Good," he said. "Now—food."

Gabriel shut the door. He heard Chigaru's footsteps going away. He'd left it unlocked, and Gabriel thought for a moment of trying to break Lucy out right now, while the door was open and Chigaru was away from his post. But it wasn't feasible—not with three stories of armed men between them and the tunnel, and not with Lucy barely steady enough to stand. With some food in her, some more time for the drugs to get out of her system... maybe. But not yet.

"I'm going to talk to Amun and get him to stop giving you the drugs," Gabriel said. "I'll tell him you're going to be cooperative now."

"Who's Amun?"

"Tall guy, goatee, fez?"

She shook her head. "Haven't met him. Have you seen Khufu yet?"

"Who's Khufu?"

"The boss around here," she said. "Calls himself 'Khufu the Second.' Like he's a pharaoh. Carries a scepter, wears a mask, this traditional Egyptian thing... He's the man in charge."

"I thought Amun was—"

"I don't know who Amun is," Lucy said, "but he's not in charge. You meet Khufu, you know he's the boss."

She lay back on the bed. Her eyes were sliding shut, though she was fighting to keep them open.

"You shouldn't have come," she said. "I don't want you hurt because of me."

"What do you mean, shouldn't have come?" He reached out and stroked her cheek. "I'm your brother. Of course I'm going to come."

"I bet Michael's mad at me," she mumbled.

"He's worried about you," Gabriel said.

"He's always worried. About everything."

"So he's more worried than normal. He cares about you, you know."

"Even though I haven't talked to him since I was seventeen?"

"Even though," Gabriel said. "You're still his sister."

Her eyes slid shut and this time they stayed shut.

"I'm glad," she said, her voice very tired, "that at least they're not asking for money. That's what I figured they wanted. And I *really* didn't want Michael paying ransom for me. You know how I feel about the money."

"Yeah, I know." Gabriel smoothed her hair. "When this is all over, maybe you can explain it to Michael. Over a nice dinner in New York."

She sleepily shook her head. "Not happening."

"Why not?" Gabriel said, but at that moment the door swung open and Chigaru entered carrying a tray.

He put it down it on the desk, glared at Gabriel, and left without a word.

There was a plate of rice, some strips of grilled chicken, a little pile of hummus. A bottle of water accompanied it.

"Try to get some down," Gabriel said—but when he turned to look at Lucy he saw she was asleep.

Well. It would keep. Hopefully she'd eat some when she woke up, maybe even a bite or two of the chicken. Not that he was too optimistic. Lucy had been a committed vegetarian since childhood.

Gabriel went over to the window. There were indeed bars attached on the outside of the glass pane. The wooden boards were screwed into the wall over them. Peering through the cracks between the boards he could just make out the bougainvillea-covered wall of the building across the street.

And what about the building they were in? Gabriel remembered his brief look at it when they'd gotten out of the limo. There was no bougainvillea here. No fire escape, no drainpipe. Nothing to hold onto or to shimmy down. Just three sheer stories of sandstone wall.

Gabriel raised the window, put his hand through the bars, and tested the strength of the boards. They seemed firmly attached. The only thing was, as Gabriel knew from caving and climbing, sandstone was soft. You could drive a piton into it barehanded if you had to, and pull it out again afterwards; whatever screws they'd used to attach these boards should come out, too, with enough force. He gave one of the boards a few blows with the heel of his hand. After three or four, he felt it loosen slightly, and after a few more it was moving noticeably. One more strike, he thought, and it would come free.

Gabriel closed the window and went back to the chair. Lucy was sitting up, chewing on a spoonful of rice.

"I thought you were asleep," he said.

"I was, till you started banging on the wall."

They heard a hand at the doorknob outside, saw it turn.

"Eat," Gabriel whispered quickly, "and rest—and be prepared to move, fast, when I come for you."

The door opened and Kemnebi stuck his head inside. He gestured to Gabriel.

"Come," he said again.

Gabriel stood. "All right. I'm going to want to talk to Amun."

"Later," Kemnebi said.

"What do you mean, later? I want to talk to him now."

"Later," the big man repeated. "Khufu awaits."

12

HE WAS LED DOWNSTAIRS TO THE GROUND FLOOR, through the living room, and into a corridor he hadn't seen before. Gabriel was struck by the sudden change of decoration in the hallway. The walls here were the color of stone and uneven, and had been painted with fairly good hand-drawn reproductions of Egyptian hieroglyphics. It was as if the Alliance wanted to give the impression of walking into a pyramid or an ancient temple. They'd even mounted torches along the way in metal holders. As the modern living room receded behind them, it felt a bit like walking back through time.

Gabriel reached out and touched one wall. It wasn't genuine stone—it felt like cast resin, painted over to look like stone.

"Do not touch," Kemnebi snapped.

"Disney's got nothing on you guys," Gabriel murmured.

They reached the end of the corridor, where the wall was painted to look like a large sandstone block. Kemnebi grabbed a concealed handhold and pulled it open. The wall swiveled toward them, revealing a chapel-sized space lit by torches. Gabriel stepped through. He suspected they were in the adjacent building now. He turned to ask—but Kemnebi pushed the section of the wall closed behind him.

Gabriel was alone.

The interior was designed to resemble the King's Chamber from an Egyptian pyramid. Gabriel had seen the real thing several times and this was not a bad facsimile. The pyramids had been built as elaborate tombs for the pharaohs, intended to provide them with a comfortable home in the afterlife, though ancient notions of comfort had never struck him as all that comfortable. You'd generally have a large throne made of a single piece of carved stone; the one here was set upon a pedestal with six steps leading up to it from the floor. You'd have your statues of Egyptian gods—here, several man-sized ones stood flanking either side of the throne and much larger ones in each corner of the room were posed as if holding up the ceiling. Smaller statuettes were scattered around, alongside pedestals bearing basins filled with water. A sarcophagus stood on the right side of the chamber, its stone cover intricately decorated with jewels and gold inlay.

"Bow, American. Bow before your pharaoh."

The voice echoed through the room. It was crisp and commanding, with a hint of a Middle-Eastern accent, but only a hint.

Gabriel moved toward the throne. He was off to one side and could see that it was still empty—and there was no one behind it, either. But as he watched, a man suddenly appeared, stepping out from a patch of shadow.

Khufu was as Lucy had described him, dressed in the vestments of an Egyptian pharaoh, from the wood-soled sandals up to the ornate *nemes*, the striped royal headdress. The *nemes* had fine accordion pleating on lappets, folds that were held to the forehead with a metal band. And below that band, covering his face, the man wore a carved mask of a falcon. Gabriel recognized it as the face of Horus, the god of pharaohs. The man also wore an ankle-length transparent robe—transparency once signified an Egyptian's wealth and importance—and beneath the robe he wore a loincloth. Aside from several gold bracelets on his arms, the rest of his sinewy body was bare. He held a golden scepter in his right hand, its head curved like a cobra about to strike.

"You shall bow to me, American," Khufu said. "Willingly or no."

Gabriel didn't move. "This is quite a display," he said, "but that's all it is. A display. Any man could build it, if he was rich enough and had a thing for King Tut. I'm not impressed."

"You are insolent," the masked man said, advancing toward him. "Amun told me it was so."

"Good," Gabriel said. "That'll save us some time."

The man leveled the end of his scepter in Gabriel's direction. "We agree: there is no point in wasting time." He gestured with the scepter—and suddenly Gabriel found himself blinded with an agonizing wave of pain.

It was as if he'd licked a finger and stuck it in an outlet. A jolt of high-voltage electricity shot through his body, making every hair stand on end and every nerve ending burn. He felt himself flung to the floor with tremendous force. He slid backwards a few feet, stunned by the charge.

Khufu stood motionless, still pointing the scepter.

What the hell was *that thing?*

He tried to stand but Khufu aimed the scepter at him again. Gabriel put his hands up before him. "Okay, okay, I get—"

Another jolt of electricity shot through him, causing every muscle in his body to clench tight as a fist. He felt it in his eyelids and the soles of his feet. He could smell his hair singe.

"Those who cultivate the seeds of disobedience," Khufu said, "reap only pain." He lowered the scepter. "Now, rise. If you can."

Gabriel slowly rolled over, groaned involuntarily, got to his hands and knees. He finally managed to stand. His entire body ached and his knees trembled.

"You are strong," Khufu said. "But no man is strong enough to withstand the fury of the gods. If I smite you once more, your innards will cook inside you, your bowels turn to water; once more again and your heart will burst. There are few worse deaths."

Gabriel didn't answer.

"I have done this to you for a reason," Khufu said. "I wish to demonstrate that you are at my mercy. You live or die by my grace."

"Consider the point made," Gabriel said.

"Good. Now, Amun tells me you have agreed to help us find the Second Stone."

"I did agree," Gabriel said. "I'm having second thoughts now."

"Don't. You should be honored to be chosen. It will be an event celebrated throughout the course of history. Your name will be forever linked to its discovery. When the new world is born out of the ashes of the old, you will have been a part of it. You should rejoice in your good fortune."

"That's all right. You can rejoice for both of us."

"Oh, I will. The Second Stone will allow me to lead Egypt into a new reign of power. First, the Middle East. Israel will bow at our feet. Saudi Arabia will acknowledge the true masters of Africa. Then the Mediterranean will be ours again. We will take back Rome and Constantinople. And finally your own distant borders will fall. Egypt *will* be the leader of the world once again."

"Well, no one can accuse you of thinking small," Gabriel said.

"The most satisfying conquest, of course, will be France. To exact revenge on the country that raped Egypt during Napoleon's reign will be the sweetest victory. Napoleon was a monster and a thief. He and his brother Louis will be visited by Anubis in the afterlife and be subjected to excruciating torment. They already reside in hell, but their existence there will be made worse still, for they will see their people kneel to us. And after the destruction of France, Britain shall fall. We will take back what they hold in their so-called *museums* and then crush their country. Two new pyramids will rise, one in Paris and one in London, to mark their subjugation."

Khufu pointed the staff at him again, and Gabriel flinched slightly. "You will cooperate. You will do as Amun says, or you will suffer pain you cannot imagine—and your sister as well. You will find the Second Stone or you will both beg for death's release."

Gabriel said nothing.

"Do you understand?"

"Yes, yes, I understand."

The two men faced each other for a moment. "I believe you do," Khufu said. "Go, then. Get the rest you require. You have much work to do beginning in the morning."

Gabriel heard the wall pivot open behind him. He had been dismissed. On unsteady legs, he walked out of the chamber. Kemnebi stood waiting—and caught him when Gabriel's legs gave out.

13

THE HUNT FOUNDATION JET WAS CAVERNOUS ENOUGH
when full. With only one person on it other than Charlie
in the cockpit, the emptiness was disquieting. Sammi
Ficatier tried to put it out of her mind. She pressed
buttons in the armrest of her seat until she found one
that dimmed the cabin lights and another that put on
some music, and then she put her head back and tried
to sleep.

But it was not to be. The music was interrupted by
the sound of a phone ringing. It kept ringing till she
found another button on the armrest labeled with a
picture of a phone and pressed it.

"Miss Ficatier?" It was Michael Hunt's voice.

"Yes?" she said, unsure whether he could hear her if
she just spoke regularly.

Apparently he could. "You promised you'd answer
my questions," Michael said. "When you had the time.
As you have a few hours ahead of you now in the air…"

"Certainly," she said. "What would you like to know?"

"How do you know my sister?"

"We took classes together in Nice," Sammi said. "We became friends."

"And my brother?"

"We… met in Cifer's apartment."

"Excuse me?"

"Cifer's apartment," Sammi said. "Lucy. Your sister."

"What are you talking about?" Michael said. "Cifer is a, is a *computer* hacker who has helped us out from time to time—what does Cifer have to do with my sister?"

"Cifer *is* your sister," Sammi said. "She hacks computers, she calls herself Cifer. I thought you knew that."

There was silence on the other end. Then the voice said, "No. I did not know that."

Sammi's heart sank. Had she just said the wrong thing? She knew Cifer didn't get along with her brother, hadn't spoken to him for years; she hadn't known he didn't even know her name. *The hell with it*, she thought. *Saving your life is more important.*

"So," Michael said, softly, "tell me what happened to my brother."

She filled him in, from the ransacked apartment in Nice and the chase by the police to the flight into Cairo and her kidnapping at the bazaar. She described how she'd escaped from the men who'd grabbed her and how she'd gotten back just in time to see Gabriel bundled first into a limousine and then into a private plane. She told him how she'd found out where the plane was headed. She didn't tell him how it had ended, with her facing the man in the control room at gunpoint and realizing there was nothing to tie him up with and no way she could trust him not to sound the alarm. She'd thought one shooting in a day, and that in self-defense, was her limit. She'd learned she was wrong.

Michael asked many questions, forcing her to double back and re-tell parts of the story. He probed for details she'd forgotten or never known. But finally his questions petered out, like a wind-up toy running down.

"And you haven't heard from Gabriel since you saw him board the plane," Michael said.

"No. Have you?"

"I'm afraid not. I tried tracking his phone—nothing. The signal's dead."

"Maybe he has it turned off?" Sammi said.

"Not this signal," Michael said. "It can't be turned off."

"Don't worry," Sammi said. "I'll find him. I'll find them both." But she heard the empty bravado in her own voice.

"Marrakesh is a big place," Michael said.

It was true—Marrakesh was large, and she'd never been there before.

"Do you maybe know anyone there who could help?" she said.

He hesitated before replying and even then seemed to be letting the words out only reluctantly. "There is… one man. I wish we had someone more reliable, but…"

"Anyone is better than no one."

"Not necessarily," Michael said. "This man… he did save my brother's life once—he hid him in his cellar for nine days when the Royal Gendarmerie were after him. And he knows the country like a native. He *is* a native."

"So what's the problem?"

"He's... Actually I don't know what I'd call him. He's a criminal, or at least he has connections to the underworld there."

"That sounds perfect," Sammi said. "The men we are trying to find are criminals too."

"His ethics leave much to be desired. He only helped us because we paid him handsomely. If someone else had offered him more..."

"Well, then, don't let anyone offer more," Sammi said. "You've got enough money, don't you?"

"Of course—the money's not important," Michael said. "If I knew for sure money was the only thing Reza cared about, we'd be fine. We can outbid pretty much anyone out there and he knows it. What worries me is that..."

"What?"

"Money's not the only thing a man like that values, Miss Ficatier. There's pride, there's fame, there's stature, power; there are sensual pleasures. Reza Arif is unpredictable, and that makes him dangerous. But he's the only person we've got in Marrakesh."

"Then I think," Sammi said, "he's our man."

MICHAEL SENT AN E-MAIL TO THE LAST ADDRESS HE had on file for Arif. To his surprise, he received a reply within a half hour. Arif supplied a telephone number and asked that Michael call him on a land line.

"Michael Hunt! As I live and breathe!" Arif bellowed jovially. "How many years has it been?"

"How are you, Reza?"

"Happy, wealthy, and in good health. And you, sir?"

"Not so well, Reza. I'm concerned about Gabriel. And Lucy. Our sister."

"Oh? What is the matter?"

Michael briefly recounted the situation for him.

"Michael, you are asking an awful lot," Arif said, his voice suddenly cagey.

"Are you saying you can't help?"

"No… not 'can't.' But—the Alliance of the Pharaohs… this is not a minor organization. Nor is it a government operative who, even when corrupt, plays by his own corrupt rules. These are killers, Michael, plain and simple. No, strike that—they are neither plain nor simple. These are killers who relish what they do and revel in making it as painful as they possibly can."

"What are you saying, Reza?"

"Merely that I would need to be well incented before I would consider tangling with them."

"You will be," Michael said.

"Let us discuss," Reza said, "just how well."

14

THEY PUT HIM IN A BEDROOM ON THE TOP FLOOR.
After picking briefly at a plate of chicken, rice, and
hummus—it might have brought to him intact from
Lucy's room—Gabriel collapsed on the bed and lay
without moving for several hours, not sleeping, just
recovering. He replayed over and over in his mind
the events in Khufu's chamber and came no closer
to understanding what had happened. It was the
scepter—it had to be, unless that was just stagecraft
and misdirection and somehow the electrical charge
had been shot up through the floor. But no—his soles
were rubber and Khufu's were wood with metal trim;
if there were any electricity running through the floor,
the pharaoh would have gotten it worse than Gabriel.

So it must have been the scepter, concealing some
sort of long-distance taser or stun gun—Gabriel did
know of batons used by police in certain situations that
delivered a similar charge. Hell, cattle prods did more

or less the same thing, and could be used to subdue humans as well as animals. Not from a distance, true... but who could say that some sort of long-range wireless electroshock weapon hadn't been developed? If one had, maybe the Alliance had gotten hold of a prototype in one of their heists...

Or maybe it was a stick that channeled the wrath of Egypt's ancient gods. Whatever it was, Gabriel knew one thing: he wanted to stay clear of it in the future.

And that meant getting out of here now.

The digital clock on the dresser told him it was four-thirty in the morning. His whole body was sore, but he forced himself to get up from the bed. He found he could walk, if somewhat stiffly; could move his arms, his fingers. He went through a routine of stretches and then took a shower, first as hot as he could stand and then as cold. When he got back into his clothes, he felt almost human.

He went to the window. Like Lucy's, it was boarded up and fitted with bars outside the pane. Glancing through the cracks between the boards he could see that the sun hadn't yet risen. Better yet, the shadowy sliver of wall he glimpsed across the way included copious bougainvillea—exactly the view he'd seen from Lucy's window, just slightly higher up, which meant this room must be directly above hers.

He opened the window and began the process of loosening the boards, hammering each swiftly with his palm. When one hand tired, he switched to the other. It took several hard blows apiece to knock out the screws holding them in, blows Gabriel was sure could be heard throughout the building. But no one showed up at his door, so maybe the sound wasn't carrying quite as much as he thought. One by one he pounded at the boards until they came free and plummeted the four stories to the street below. He could hear the distant cracks as the wood splintered.

Next, Gabriel tested the strength of the bars. These were fastened more snugly. He moved the desk till it was directly below the window, lay on his back with his heels against the bars, and began methodically kicking at them. He felt them budge, first just a bit, then a bit more. He redoubled his effort. One by one, they came loose. He stopped short of kicking them out, though—the noise of a steel bar landing on the pavement from four stories up would wake everyone for sure. Instead, he worked each bar the last few millimeters by hand, wrenching it out and carefully pulling it back inside. He laid the first three bars quietly on the desk, then stowed the last one in his inside jacket pocket.

Having cleared away the last barrier, he stuck his head out through the window and looked down. As he'd remembered: a smooth, straight shot down to the street. He would need rappelling rope of some kind.

Gabriel looked around the bedroom for something that might work. The cable on the television wasn't long enough. He didn't have enough clothing to tie together. His eyes landed on the bed. Sometimes the old ways were the best.

He yanked off the thin bedspread and the lower and upper sheets. He tied them to one another with secure sailors' knots. Unfortunately, even tied corner to corner diagonally, the combined length was only around eighteen feet. Not enough to get down to the ground.

But—it was enough to get down to Lucy's window. One step at a time.

As quietly as he could, Gabriel pushed the bed across the floor so that it butted against the windowed wall.

He then twisted the top sheet and tied one end to the leg of bed closest to the window. He tugged on the knot to make sure it would hold, then tugged once more on each of the other knots for good measure. Having satisfied himself that they were secure, or at least as secure as they were going to get, he tossed the loose end out the window. Gabriel positioned himself on the bed and crawled out backwards, his legs dangling in the air. He put his weight on the rope slowly, cautiously. It held. He found the surface of the wall with his feet, planted his soles firmly. Clasping the sheet-rope tightly with both hands, he began to descend.

Rappelling to Lucy's window only took him onto the second of the two sheets. The bedspread still extended below, not quite reaching to the second floor.

Looking down, he saw the pavement far below. The broken remnants of the boards were a fine reminder of how much damage a fall from this height could do.

Speaking of which—

He released the sheet with one hand and worked his fingers under the edge of the board outside Lucy's window that he had loosened earlier. He pried it off the rest of the way and let it fall. Now he could see in through the window. The room was dark—but he could make out Lucy's shape, curled up in the bed. He tapped lightly against the glass. No movement. Rapped again, a little louder. Still nothing.

Wake up!

The drugs, he figured; even if they hadn't dosed her again, whatever was still in her system was probably making her sleep more soundly than usual. And if they *had* dosed her again…

He knocked as loudly as he dared. This time it elicited a response. The humped shape moved on the bed, turning over. He knocked again. She sat up.

Holding on to the sheet-rope with one arm and his twined ankles, Gabriel pried another board off the soft sandstone. He tapped once more. She turned toward the sound, saw him, and ran to the window, flinging it open. She was dressed in a long T-shirt, her legs and feet bare. She seemed fairly alert, though still a bit muzzy—or perhaps just bewildered at having been awaked by the sight of her brother dangling on bedsheets outside her window.

"Gabriel! How did you get out there?"

"They put me in the room above you. Come on." He pried the remaining board loose and let it fall. "I'll need your help to get these bars off. My leverage isn't so good from here."

He passed her the metal bar from his pocket and instructed her to use it as a lever. She wedged it between two of the bars, gripped the free end in both hands, and pulled. She may have been small and she may have been thin—but she wasn't weak. The bar she was trying to loosen shifted with a groan of metal against stone. Gabriel helped her with his free hand. Soft sandstone powder spilled out of the holes around the screws. He held onto the bar as it came free so it wouldn't fall, and Lucy carefully brought it inside. They repeated the performance with the others.

In five minutes it was done. Gabriel threw a leg over the sill and climbed inside, leaving the sheet-rope dangling behind him.

"Come on, help me take the sheets off your bed," he said. Then he changed his mind. "No, I'll do it. You get dressed. Hurry."

Gabriel removed the sheets and bedspread, tied them together, and then pulled his line in from the window. He tied the new set onto the old and then threw the entire assembly outside. Gabriel looked down and saw that the end was just above the top of the first floor. That was good enough. The drop to the ground from there shouldn't be too dangerous.

Lucy was dressed and ready to go.

"How do you feel? Did they drug you again?"

She shook her head. "Not since yesterday."

Gabriel gestured to the window. "You think you can climb down?"

"With my eyes cl—"

She was interrupted by a knock on the door. They froze. "Hey," came a voice. "What's going on in there?" They heard the sound of a key in the lock. Turning.

Gabriel bolted for the bathroom and flattened himself against the wall. Lucy moved quickly to the door and stood beside it with one hand on the knob, preventing it from opening it too widely.

The face at the door belonged to Chigaru.

"Wait!" Lucy said, pushing back on the door so that there was only a narrow opening. She stuck her head around the edge. "I'm not dressed!"

"I heard something," Chigaru said.

"I fell out of bed," Lucy said.

"It sounded like voices," he said.

"Yeah, that was me cursing," Lucy said, "when I fell out of bed. Would you please leave me alone, Chigaru?"

Chigaru put one hand on the door, forced his thick fingers inside. "I'm going to take a look around."

"I told you, I'm not dressed. Stay out!"

But he shoved his way in. And the first thing he saw was that she was completely dressed.

"What's going on?" he said, his voice loud, angry. "I'll make you tell me—" He raised an arm to backhand her across the face. But he found himself unable to lower it.

He looked over at the man who'd seized his wrist in a steel grip.

"Close the door," Gabriel told his sister.

As Lucy did, he squeezed tighter, his thumb on the inside of Chigaru's wrist.

Chigaru's face showed a mixture of pain and fear—like he wanted to cry out for help, but some last ounce of pride kept him from doing so.

"You are *dead*, Hunt. You and your whore sister." He grimaced as Gabriel increased the pressure further. The pain drove him to his knees. "You won't get away with this," he hissed through clenched teeth. "Khufu will kill you."

"Maybe so," Gabriel said. "But not tonight." Reaching over to the desk, he hefted one of the metal bars they'd removed from the window. Chigaru saw it and finally opened his mouth to scream—but Gabriel brought the bar down across his temple and Chigaru went out like a snuffed candle.

Gabriel dropped the bar and the man's wrist. "Go," he told Lucy. "I'll be right behind you."

While Lucy climbed onto the windowsill, Gabriel stooped to search Chigaru. He found a wallet and took out the few bills it contained in local currency. "Sorry, pal." Patting him down further, Gabriel felt a bulky item in the man's jacket pocket—a gun? He reached inside and almost shouted as he pulled the object out. It was his Colt .45! Gabriel gave it a kiss on the barrel and stuck it in his waistband.

He went to the window. Lucy had already gone eight feet or so, letting herself down hand over hand.

"When you get to the bottom," Gabriel whispered,

"drop and roll. *Drop and roll,* understand? I don't want you to break your leg."

Lucy didn't answer; he didn't know if she'd heard. But she kept going. All he could do was hope.

He looked back at the door, at Chigaru's unconscious form on the floor beside the bed. How long would it be before one of the other guards wondered where he was? Or till someone else heard something?

He was tempted to climb out and start his descent, too—but he didn't want to put any weight on the sheets until she was all the way down.

He watched her go, shimmying down the line like a pro. When she made it to the bottom, she let go, dropped, and rolled. Perfect.

He tugged on the sheets to test their strength again, then slipped out the window.

He started to rappel hastily—but he hadn't gone more than a few feet when he heard a voice shouting above him.

Gabriel looked up. The head of one of Amun's men was sticking out of the window on the top floor. The man shouted again, sounding the alarm. Then he whipped out a knife and began slicing at the sheets.

They wouldn't hold—Gabriel knew a few strokes with a sharp blade would sever the fabric. And he was still too high up to fall safely. Gabriel thought fast. He reached into his sock and grabbed the kitchen knife he'd stolen in Cairo. Holding it firmly in one fist, he rammed the blade into the soft sandstone as hard as he could. The impact jarred his wrist and he had to bite down on a yelp of pain—but the knife stuck. At that very moment, the sheets cut loose. Gabriel held on to the knife handle with one clenched fist, clinging to the wall by this narrowest of handholds. By comparison, the rubber-clad pickaxe handle in Carlsbad Caverns had been a luxury.

As the sheet-rope tumbled past him, Gabriel managed to snag it with his other arm. He let it run through his fingers till he found the end, then swung it up and over, wrapping the twisted sheet as tightly as he could several times around the knife's handle. It wasn't pretty, and when he was done he didn't have a knot. But the handle of the knife did have a decorative curve that was enough to keep the coiled-up sheet from slipping off altogether. It would have to do—already he could feel the knife's blade starting to come out of the widening crevice, and inside the building the sounds of shouts and clattering feet were multiplying. Gabriel took a deep breath and let go of the knife, sliding as fast as he dared down the sheet.

Looking up, he saw the knife handle slowly tilt downwards.

Seconds later, the blade pulled out of the wall.

He fell the last dozen feet to the bottom, landing in a painful crouch.

"What happened to 'drop and roll'?" Lucy demanded, bending close to him and helping him stand.

He grabbed her hand.

"*Run*," he said.

15

DAWN WAS BREAKING, AND THE DJEMAA EL FNA WAS already awake.

The melodic, soulful morning prayers boomed over loudspeakers mounted high on poles throughout the square. It was standard procedure to broadcast them in nearly every major city in Morocco. Gabriel and Lucy ran past dozens of workers and tradesmen, shopkeepers and vendors and performers, all bowing close to the ground. A few looked up as they passed, more as the Alliance guards came running after them moments later.

There were no tourists in the square yet, and no workers at work. As soon as the prayers were completed it would be swarmed by people beginning their day, a crowd among which Gabriel and Lucy might lose themselves. But while the sacred ritual was taking place, they could be seen from blocks away.

"We need somewhere to hide," he said, taking a

corner and pulling Lucy after him. "We can't stay out in the open."

Lucy pointed to a side street where a number of carts, wagons, vans, and cars were parked. "Over there."

They ran. But after his ordeal the previous day, Gabriel was finding himself short of breath and hurting, and he knew Lucy was probably feeling similar following her period of drugged captivity. Behind them, he heard running footsteps drawing near. He glanced back. Their pursuers weren't in sight yet—but they weren't going to be able to make it to the side street before they were.

Gabriel pulled Lucy into an alcove beside a shop whose window display showed bulging sacks of grain and cereal. Two Alliance men appeared an instant latter, running at full speed. Gabriel and Lucy pressed themselves back against the stone wall. The men sprinted past without breaking stride.

Once they'd gone, Gabriel pulled the picks out of his belt and made quick work of the lock on the shop's door. No alarm went off, thankfully, and he and Lucy entered, re-locking the door behind them and walking quickly to the rear of the space. They crouched behind a tall stack of burlap bags. Gabriel held his finger to his lips. They heard the men returning, panting, talking to each other furiously in Arabic. He understood only every tenth word, but the general tenor of the conversation was easy enough to guess: *Where did they go? They must be hiding!*

They tried the door, rattling the knob. Then a muttered curse came from one of the men, followed by the sound of departing footsteps.

Gabriel waited a full two minutes before slowly raising his head over the grain sacks. He couldn't see much from where they were, but the little he could see suggested that the men were at least not waiting for them directly outside. He motioned for Lucy to stay where she was and crept to the front of the store in a low crouch. He scanned the area from every angle the store's front window permitted. Nothing. They seemed to be safe for the moment.

He returned to Lucy and dropped heavily to the floor beside her.

"They're gone. For now."

"So what do we do? You have a plan?"

"No," he said.

Her brow wrinkled. "You're joking, right?"

"I'll think of something," he said.

"At least we're out of the Casa del Khufu," she said. "I was getting pretty tired of that place."

The loudspeakers went quiet. The morning prayers were over.

"There'll be people all over the place in a few minutes," Gabriel said. "We can stay in here till it's crowded and then slip out and blend in."

"Neither of us is exactly the blending type," Lucy said.

Gabriel thought of Sammi, tucking her red hair under a headscarf at the bazaar in Cairo. "We'll do the best we can."

"We need to get out of the city," Lucy said.

"And to a phone," he said, scanning the area around the store's front counter for one. There was none in sight. Apparently, like many people in this part of the world, the shopkeeper relied on his mobile. "If I can reach Michael, he can get us on a plane. I want to try Sammi again, too."

"Sammi?" Lucy asked. "My Sammi? What are you talking about?"

Too late, he realized he hadn't told her that part of the story before. "She came with me to Cairo, from Nice."

"What were you doing in Nice?"

"I went to your apartment. Wanted to see if I could find any sign of where they'd taken you."

"And Sammi...?"

"She was doing the same thing," Gabriel said. "She insisted on coming along."

"So... what happened?" Gabriel could hear the fear in her voice.

"I don't know. We agreed she'd follow me from a distance when I went to meet the Alliance. But we lost contact in Cairo." He didn't tell her that Amun had said she'd been captured, maybe killed. Even if it was true, Lucy didn't need to hear it right now. "She's probably still in Cairo, wondering what the hell happened to me."

"Why did you let her come with you?"

He held up his hands. "I tried to stop her. She's a stubborn girl. Just like you."

A thin smile appeared on Lucy's face, but it didn't stay there long. "I hope she's okay."

"Me, too," Gabriel said. "I want you both somewhere safe while I take care of this business with the Alliance."

"What 'business'?"

"They found you in Nice—they won't stop hunting just because you've gone somewhere else. Not now. They've got a score to settle now. Besides," Gabriel said, "if that stone's out there like they said, I can't just let it fall into their hands."

"Why? For god's sake, Gabriel, what does it matter who's got some old stone? Haven't you got enough old stones already?"

"Not one like this," Gabriel said. "Not if what they said about it is true."

She shrugged, let her eyes slide shut. "All right. Do what you have to," she said.

"What," Gabriel said, "you're not going to insist on coming with me?"

"Not a chance," Lucy said. "I just want to get the hell out of here."

IT DIDN'T TAKE LONG FOR PEOPLE TO START FILLING the square. Gabriel heard the first loud calls that indicated the water sellers had arrived. Sounds of shops opening and people greeting each other.

The door to the grain shop opened and, peeking up from behind the sacks, Gabriel saw the shopkeeper put down a bag and strap on an apron. The first customers entered directly behind him, a pair of women in Moroccan dress, followed by a gray-haired husband and wife with matching cameras around their necks. Gabriel and Lucy stood as the couple walked past and casually exited the store behind them.

The sun was bright now and the square was full. The same complement of acrobats, musicians, mendicants and food sellers were in place and at work. A pair of early morning tour buses had parked nose-to-tail on the less populated side of the square and were disgorging passengers dressed in knee-length shorts and shirts with resort logos printed across the front. They fanned themselves with folded pamphlets, sweating already even though the real heat of the day was still hours away.

Lucy blinked in the glare and ran her fingers through her hair, which was standing up in spiky green clumps.

"You want me to blend in," she muttered.

"Come on."

They walked toward the group of tourists behind the nearer of the buses. A Moroccan guide was speaking to them through an electric megaphone.

"We are now going into the older portion of the Djemaa el Fna. Please to walk along this side of the square. We will stay another thirty minutes. Please to buy what beautiful souvenirs you find. Please to return to the bus by nine o'clock. As soon as everyone is back we will leave and travel to the beautiful Majorelle Garden."

Gabriel and Lucy merged into the crowd, most of whom appeared to be American judging by their accents.

"Can't we just get a taxi?" Lucy whispered.

"I'm afraid all the money we've got is what your friend Chigaru had in his wallet. And the Alliance doesn't seem to pay its people very well." On the plane ride into Morocco, Amun had made Gabriel empty his pockets—less, Gabriel figured, as a matter of theft than to reduce his mobility if somehow he managed to get away. It was working.

The tour group stopped at a basket shop, a jewelry shop; they spent some time at a fruit stand. Then they walked toward a familiar street. At the far end Gabriel saw a sign that brought him up short—*Nizan's Carpets*.

"Let's slip away, Lucy. Slowly and quietly."

But it was too late. Nizan stood in front of the shop, one hand raised to greet the morning's customers. His eyes fell on Gabriel, and his smile abruptly vanished. He turned and shouted something in Arabic toward the back of the shop.

"Go. *Go*," Gabriel said, pushing Lucy into motion. They took off across the square, threading between the knots of tourists and muttering apologies on the run for the occasional collision. The square was crowded enough already at this hour that it was difficult to move with any speed. The only good thing about the congestion was that it made things equally hard for their pursuers.

Gabriel looked back. Kemnebi and two other men had come out of the carpet shop. Nizan pointed in Gabriel's direction.

Gabriel pulled Lucy toward the section where the crowd was thickest, a wall of people facing one direction, watching something. Lucy speared right through them, slipping between a pair of men holding their cameras up to their eyes. Gabriel followed. He stumbled into an open area, in the center of which a performer was busy—

Charming snakes.

The man, wearing an open vest over his skinny frame and a turban on his head, held several serpents in his arms. At his feet several more were coiled—a couple of cobras, a viper, an asp. He sang to the reptiles in a high-pitched voice that Gabriel thought would be enough to make him take a bite out of the guy if he were a snake, but the snakes appeared to be entranced by it.

Lucy had plunged into the circle at top speed and it took her a few steps to come to a halt. She caught herself up, arms windmilling to keep her from falling forward. There was a cobra at her feet. It twisted to face her and hissed. She reflexively stepped sideways, bumping into the covered basket by the charmer's side. The man jumped up, shouting, reaching for it, but not in time. The lid toppled off and the basket went over, spilling its contents.

Suddenly there were two dozen snakes on the ground, spreading in every direction. The crowd shrank back with a collective intake of breath. Two people screamed and several bolted for safety, though most stayed frozen in place. A few were snapping photos as quickly as they could.

Lucy, meanwhile, had snakes on every side of her—she couldn't take a step without coming within striking distance of at least one.

"Don't move," Gabriel said. He came closer, watching the snakes carefully. He'd have thought the charmer would have milked their venom before putting them in the basket—but betting on that could be a deadly proposition.

The big cobra was still the one closest to Lucy. Gabriel circled around till he was beside it, then aimed a careful kick at its raised head with the toe of his boot. It went flying. The crowd scurried out of its way, and it landed hissing.

Gabriel took hold of another snake—an asp— behind its head just as it darted toward Lucy's leg. He flung it aside. "Here," he called, reaching out an arm. Lucy leaped toward him and he snatched her off her feet, carrying her over the snakes between them. One reared up and snapped at her heels, but its jaws closed on air. Lucy clasped her arms around her brother's neck and Gabriel ran, not putting her down till they were a safe distance away.

"Are you okay? Can you walk?"

Her eyes were wide with fear, but she nodded. Gabriel let her go and they took off. They carefully skirted the edge of another circle of tourists. This one appeared to be watching nothing more venomous than a troupe of acrobats—but you never knew what else might be going on in the center of the circle, and one encounter with the local wildlife was enough for any morning.

Gabriel tried to keep an eye out for the Alliance men, but it was impossible in this chaos. Occasionally he'd glimpse a familiar scowling face or a raised arm with a gun in it, but he was sure there were other men, equally dangerous, that he wasn't spotting. They, on the other hand, wouldn't be having much trouble keeping an eye on him and Lucy. The only thing he could do was keep pushing toward the edge, toward a place where they could hide, or a car they could use to get away—

Suddenly, a hand reached between a pair of people behind them and took hold of Gabriel's shoulder. He tried to shake free, but it clung mercilessly. From the weight, he'd have bet money—if he'd had any money worth betting—that it was Kemnebi's.

Gabriel bent at the knees and spun, launching a punch behind him. It collided with the rock-hard boulder of flesh that was Kemnebi's midsection.

The big man reached in and encircled Gabriel with his arms, ignoring the punch as if it had been a pat from a child. He lifted Gabriel off his feet and began constricting, squeezing Gabriel's chest with the strength of an automobile crusher. Gabriel couldn't breathe—he felt as if his ribcage was about to snap. He kicked wildly, hoping to land a blow on one or both of Kemnebi's kneecaps, but it was no use. The man was holding Gabriel so high that his legs dangled in the air.

"Let him go!" Lucy shouted, throwing punches of her own at Kemnebi's side. He kicked her aside, sending her sprawling.

The pain was excruciating. Gabriel imagined the top of his head bursting from the pressure. Looking around, he couldn't see Lucy anymore. He hoped it meant she was taking advantage of the situation to get away, at least.

He wrenched from side to side, desperately trying to pull free. In his head, he was running through his dwindling options. He couldn't get to his gun, not with his arms pinned to his sides. A head butt? It was likely to do more damage to Gabriel than to Kemnebi, whose forehead looked about as tender and vulnerable as a cinderblock. Gabriel opened his jaws wide and was about to bend forward, aiming for the cartilage of the man's nose, when suddenly Kemnebi screamed and released him.

As Gabriel fell to the ground, he saw Kemnebi's hands shoot up to his throat, which seemed to have something wrapped around it...

Lucy ran up to Gabriel, tossing aside the wicker basket she'd been carrying. It looked familiar—and now that Gabriel took a second glance, so did the thing around Kemnebi's throat. One of the charmer's snakes. Another seemed to have sunk its fangs into the back of his shirt, and more were writhing around his feet.

Lucy's face was bloodless and her hands were shaking. Gabriel had never minded snakes himself, but he knew she hated them—absolutely *hated* them. He knew what it had meant for her to go get that basket.

"Thanks," Gabriel said, climbing to his feet. "Now let's get out of here."

He took her by the arm and dragged her toward an alleyway he'd spotted earlier. It had looked promisingly dark and empty of people. Unfortunately, it also turned out to be a dead end. Gabriel glanced back. If they stayed here, it wouldn't be long before the Alliance's men would find them; on the other hand, returning to the center of the square wouldn't exactly keep them hidden either.

He looked around. Near the mouth of the alley there was a truck parked half on and half off the curb, with a wooden animal trailer hitched behind it. Gabriel went to the rear of the trailer and peered through the slats.

Inside, animals were quietly bleating.

Goats. At least half a dozen of them.

The doors on the trailer weren't locked. Gabriel turned the handle, opened the door, and held it open. "After you," he said.

"Ah, hell, Gabriel—" Lucy hesitantly put a foot up. The trailer floor was covered in filthy straw and the animals stank.

"If you could handle snakes," Gabriel said, "you can handle goats." He pushed her inside, climbed in behind her, and shut the door.

"Gabriel!"

"Sh."

He pulled her deeper into the trailer and squatted against the back wall. The goats were agitated, milling about in the constricted space and bleating angrily at the intruders. But they'd calm down. He hoped.

The smell really was overpowering. He breathed through his mouth and gestured silently to Lucy that she should do the same.

She started to say something in response, but from outside came the sound of men running into the alleyway and past the truck. The men reached the dead end, swore, and came back. Through the slats in the trailer Gabriel saw Kemnebi pass–apparently he'd gotten the better of the snakes, which must have been milked after all.

Gabriel held a finger to his lips and Lucy nodded. They both knew what was at stake.

A shadow darkened as someone approached the trailer.

Gabriel slid down until he was lying on the foul straw. He pulled Lucy down on top of him, and with the toe of one boot he nudged the leg of the nearest goat. The animal bleated complainingly but walked in the direction Gabriel had prodded it, which put its body between the side of the trailer and where Gabriel and Lucy were lying.

They waited in silence, Lucy stretched out along the length of him, her face buried in his shoulder. He stroked the back of her head with one hand. With the other, he reached slowly for his gun.

But the shadow departed, and with it came the sound of heavy footsteps moving off. They probably hadn't actually seen Gabriel and Lucy come down this particular alley; they must have had several more to search.

After a minute had passed without their hearing the men return, Gabriel helped Lucy sit up and then rose himself. "Let's give it just a little longer," he whispered to her, "then we can get—"

But at that instant someone started the truck's engine.

They both put hands out against the trailer's walls to brace themselves as the truck lurched into motion.

"Gabriel!"

"Sh." Gabriel crept forward and looked out through the slats at the farthest end, but he couldn't see who was driving the truck, or where they were headed.

The one thing he did know was that they were leaving the Djemaa el Fna.

He returned to where Lucy was half standing and gestured for her to sit again.

"But we've got to get out of here," she whispered fiercely.

"That's exactly what we're doing," Gabriel whispered back.

16

SAMMI WAS RELIEVED TO FINALLY STEP OFF THE plane at Marrakesh's Menara International Airport. She was grateful that Michael had put the plane at her disposal; she only wished she could have gotten in sooner. Enough time had passed that she feared she may have lost Gabriel's trail for good.

Her instructions from Michael were to meet Reza Arif at Baggage Claim. She had little idea what he looked like, since Michael had given her only a cursory description; and she assumed he'd given a similarly cursory description of her to Arif. Which left her wandering back and forth along the luggage retrieval claim belts, staring questioningly at the solitary men she passed and seeing no sign of recognition from any of them. She was on her fourth pass when she heard a male voice behind her.

"Mademoiselle Ficatier?"

She turned to see a handsome man in his mid-forties

with black hair and a black beard, neatly trimmed. He wore dark sunglasses, and was dressed in well-tailored clothing, a crisp bespoke suit with a crimson triangle of handkerchief showing at his breast pocket. For all that he seemed to be attempting to convey class and sophistication, though, Sammi was instantly struck with a different impression, one of menace. It was something in his eyes, the way he held himself. This was a dangerous man. She was confident she would have thought so even if Michael hadn't warned her about him.

"Yes?"

"I am Reza Arif. I am most pleased to make your acquaintance." He bowed slightly and extended his hand. "You must call me Reza."

"Sammi." She took the man's hand and shook it briefly. He clung to her fingers for an instant before letting her go.

"Are you hungry?" he asked. "Do you want something to eat or drink?"

"No, thanks. I had something in Cairo."

"Ah, yes. Fine food in Cairo. Not as fine as we have here, but… if you are not hungry, you are not hungry. No luggage?" She held up her carry-on, the small gym bag she'd brought along with her from Nice. He offered to take it from her, but she shook her head. "All right. Follow me please."

He led her to the parking garage, took out a key fob and pressed a button. A black BMW X6 beeped and flashed its lights.

He removed the sunglasses in the car. His eyes were dark, nicely setting off his swarthy skin. *He might be dangerous, but that didn't mean he wasn't attractive.* "It is not much of a disguise," he said as he put the glasses away, "but it is sufficient for the Baggage Claim at the airport." He didn't speak again until they were on the highway headed for the city. "I have been looking into this Alliance of the Pharaohs that our mutual friend mentioned."

"And?"

"It is a very difficult organization about which to uncover any information. I have many contacts in the so-called underworld, and I spent most of last night trying to get one of them to tell me something— anything—about this Alliance. I had very little luck. On the other hand, it has only been one night. Perhaps I will find something yet."

"Nobody knew anything?"

"The only piece of useful intelligence I obtained so far is that the Alliance is believed to use carpet vendors as a front—here, in Cairo, and elsewhere. Their headquarters is allegedly near the Djemaa el Fna—have you ever been…?"

"I've never been to Marrakesh."

"Ah, such a pity. I only wish you had come sometime when you had less on your mind. It is a beautiful city, and you are a beautiful woman."

Sammi said nothing. No point in encouraging him— but she also didn't want to make an enemy of him.

"I would have enjoyed giving you the grand tour. Alas, I can no longer enjoy it as I once did myself. I must remain… unnoticed."

"Why?"

"Surely our friend told you."

"Told me what?"

He shrugged expressively, his hands briefly lifting off the steering wheel. "I am supposed to be an international criminal. At least that is what I have been branded." He looked over at her and grinned. "Do not worry," he said. "I am not the villain they make me out to be. It is what you would call 'guilt by association.' I think that is the correct term. I happen to know many criminals. I have done business with them. That does not necessarily make me one, does it?"

"Not necessarily," Sammi said. "Are you one?"

He dismissed the idea with a wave of his hand. "The truth is beside the point. They would gladly imprison me if they caught me, so whatever I am or am not, I must live as if I were a criminal. I make my home in the mountains now." He pointed toward the horizon. Sammi could see the ruddy silhouette of the range in the distance. "It is a simple life. I have no complaints."

"Is it dangerous for you to come into Marrakesh?"

"Only if I am recognized by a policeman." He laughed. "Don't worry. I visit the city all the time. I just have to be careful."

Sammi couldn't see how driving a car this conspicuous and dressing in an outfit that was the car's sartorial equivalent counted as being careful. But he apparently knew what he was doing. She didn't see any police cars in the rear-view mirror.

Perhaps, she thought, he paid them off, splitting with them the bounty from the Hunt Foundation.

"We will go to the Djemaa el Fna," Arif said, "and together we shall visit each carpet store. Of course, searching every carpet store in Marrakesh is a bit like searching every boîte and café in your country. A daunting task, eh? But perhaps we will be lucky and find the right one before our friend's siblings come to a bad end."

And he smiled at her, in a way that was clearly meant to be reassuring. Instead, it left her with the distinct sense that this man had something up his handsomely tailored sleeve.

But she needed his help.

"Sounds like a plan," Sammi said.

THE TRUCK TOOK THE BETTER PART OF A HALF HOUR to get out of Marrakesh. As the road became rougher, the trailer rattled and bounced with increasing vigor, troubling the goats into louder and more nearly continuous bleating.

"How much longer do you think?" Lucy asked, keeping her voice low.

Gabriel looked out between the slats. "We're in the desert," he reported. "Nothing for miles. We're not stopping anytime soon."

"What do you say we get out," Lucy said. "Just kick open the doors and jump. Every goat for himself."

"Not here," Gabriel said. They were in the middle of nowhere, with no landmarks he could recognize. Not a place you wanted to wander on foot.

"Remember the food they gave me," Lucy said, "that rice and hummus?" Gabriel nodded. "It was terrible," she said. "Practically inedible. But right about now, I wish I'd eaten more of it."

"There're some carrots over there." Gabriel gestured to a trampled pile in one corner. One of the goats was nosing at it.

"Thanks a whole lot."

"Salad," Gabriel said. "I don't think they'll mind sharing."

"Want to bet?"

She settled back into the straw and let her eyes slide shut.

* * *

AN HOUR LATER, THEY FELT THE TRUCK TURN ONTO A
pitted dirt road. The ride became even bumpier.
Gabriel peered outside. After several minutes of
bone-jarring bounces, the worst of which threatened
to overturn the trailer, Gabriel said, "I see something.
Looks like a farm."

The truck pulled to a stop on a barren driveway
next to a farmhouse whose walls and roof were made
of lashed-together planks of wood with whitish
mortar sealing the cracks in between. An angled
roof cast a bit of shadow, just enough to shade one
side of the trailer. Chickens wandered freely across
the ground, clucking and bobbing their heads. More
goats were penned in a wooden corral. A woman
wearing a *niqab* stood beside the corral, tossing feed
to the birds. She greeted the driver in a language
Gabriel didn't understand—Berber?—when the man
got out of the truck.

"I don't suppose they've got a shower," Lucy
muttered.

The driver and the woman had a brief conversation
and then the driver went inside the house.

Lucy took the opportunity to rise to a crouch and
press her way to the back of the trailer, shoving goats
aside. She raised the metal bar holding the doors
closed, swung them to either side and dropped to the
ground. Gabriel followed close behind.

The woman let go of her canvas sack of feed and
called for the driver in a voice that rang with fear. The
driver came running out of the house. He grabbed a long-
handled hoe that was leaning against the doorframe.

"It's all right!" Gabriel called, first in English, then

152

in French, his palms extended outward, open and empty. "We're friendly."

Lucy said something as well. Gabriel couldn't understand a word of it, but the driver's stance relaxed a bit, and he answered her warily in the same tongue.

"When did you learn Berber?" Gabriel whispered.

"Had some time on my hands a couple of years back," Lucy said. "My cellmate spoke it."

"Your cellmate?" Gabriel said, but she was walking away from him, toward the farmer and what he could only guess was the man's wife.

"I've told him we're not goat thieves," she called back to Gabriel, in between exchanges in the desert language. "That we're escaping from a gang of Egyptians who were trying to kill us. They don't like Egyptians much around here."

The woman spoke rapidly to the man, who hurried past Gabriel and grabbed hold of a goat that had jumped down from the trailer. He hefted it back up and inside, then shoved the doors closed.

The woman beckoned for them to come inside the house.

"I told her we wanted to get washed, maybe have some food," Lucy said. "I said we didn't have much money but that you'd give them what you had."

"Of course." Gabriel took Chigaru's meager store of *dirham* from his pocket and pressed the crumpled bills into the man's hands. "If you can get their names, when we get out of this I'll tell Michael to send them—"

Lucy shook her head. "I told you, I won't touch that money."

"You wouldn't be touching it, they would—" But Gabriel stopped when he saw the look on her face. It was a look he remembered well from when she was a girl, a look that said she wouldn't be budged.

The woman led them into the farmhouse while her husband unloaded the goats and herded them into the corral. She showed them to a primitive but functional shower, with a pair of tin buckets suspended on a rod and a rope to tip the water out through holes punched in the buckets' sides. Gabriel saw Lucy's eyes light up and invited her to use it first. He walked off a bit to get the lay of the land and stretch his tight muscles. By the time he returned, she was bundled up in a coarse towel, her hair dripping and her clothes laid out to dry on a rock in the sun.

"All yours," she said.

He began unbuttoning his shirt. As he pulled it off, he saw Lucy staring. He looked down. "What?"

She came forward, traced a finger along one of the scars on his arm. It had come from a sword; there was a matching scar on the opposite side where the tip of the blade had come out. "Got that one in Giza," he said softly. "Inside the Great Sphinx." She moved on to a puckered knot of flesh on his side, from a bullet wound that had never healed properly. "Botswana," he said in answer to her unspoken question. She traced a thin line running crookedly from his navel to his hip. "Ninety-third Street," he said, "and Central Park West."

She patted him gently on his side. "Take your shower," she said. "I'll get us some food."

THEY SAT IN THE MODEST FARMHOUSE AT A TABLE that appeared to be made from a single cross-section cut from a huge tree, sharing a platter of dense Moroccan bread and bowls of thick vegetable soup. Lucy scarfed down three bowls.

"They don't have a telephone," she said between spoonfuls. "But they can drive us to the airport."

Gabriel dug into his pocket and took out the piece of paper onto which he'd copied the Arabic word he had seen underlined on the map in Amun's office. "Can you ask them if they know what this means?"

Lucy passed it to the man and spoke to him. The man nodded, uttered a few words. "Darif says it's Arabic. It means 'the web.' Why? Is it important?"

Gabriel took the slip of paper back. "I don't know," he said. "Just trying to figure out what we're dealing with."

The man—Darif—stood and gestured toward the door.

"He wants to know if you're ready to go," Lucy said.

Gabriel hauled himself to his feet, ignoring the dull pain in his legs, his side, his chest. "Always," he said.

REZA ARIF PARKED THE BMW NEAR THE DJEMAA EL Fna and came around to Sammi's side to open the door for her. It struck her as an exaggerated gesture, a caricature of Middle Eastern courtliness, but she let him indulge himself. Anything that kept her on his good side.

Arif led her to the heart of the busy square, pointing out buildings and regaling her with their history as they went. She tried to keep her eyes out for Gabriel or for either of the men she'd seen hustling him into the black car back in Cairo, but the crowd was too dense, too constantly in motion—a sea of heads and bodies and outstretched arms, every third one attempting to press something into her hands: a brass cup, a folded shawl, a painted vase. She shook her head at each offer and kept moving.

"There, do you see?" Arif said, pointing. "In that very building the famous British film director Alfred Hitchcock stood while making—" He turned in place, noticing that Sammi was no longer beside him. An old man with a yellowish beard trailing down the front of his robe had seized her wrist and, with his other hand, had begun to inscribe the outlines of a henna tattoo on her forearm.

"I don't want—" Sammi was saying, but the man was shaking his head and intently ignoring her.

"The lady said she does not want," Arif said, his voice suddenly cold, and the old man, looking to the side, saw the narrow blade of a stiletto by his throat. He dropped Sammi's wrist and backed off. The stiletto vanished again into Arif's sleeve.

"Stay close," he said. "Not every old man is harmless here."

Nor every young man, Sammi wanted to say. But she held her tongue and stayed by Arif's side.

They spent the next hour entering carpet shops, of which there were any number in and around the square. The eighth—or was it the ninth?—had a sign identifying the proprietor as Nizan. The couple entered and was greeted warmly by the owner himself, who took note of Reza Arif's expensive suit and immediately turned on the hard-sell reserved for tourists he believed to be wealthy. Arif answered him in Arabic while Sammi wandered around the shop, looking for any sign that Gabriel might have been here. She saw nothing to indicate one way or the other. The other seven—or was it eight?—shops had been the same. Sammi was starting to wonder if she'd even recognize a sign if she saw one. But she'd have ample opportunity to find out—there were half a dozen more shops to go.

* * *

UNSEEN BY HER, A MAN WITH A BADLY BRUISED JAW peered through a partly closed curtain and watched as Sammi walked the aisles. He smiled to himself, but it was a bitter smile with nothing of pleasure to it.

It was her—the French woman, the one who had shot his brother in cold blood. His fist clenched around the fabric of the curtain. He would have his revenge. He turned to the man beside him and explained in a few words who he'd seen.

"But Naeem," the other man said, his voice low, "Amun clearly said we are not to kill this one if we should see her—"

"Kill her?" Naeem stroked the bruise along his jaw. "I said nothing about *killing* her."

"Let's go," Sammi said, taking hold of Arif's sleeve. Through the fabric she could feel the handle of the stiletto. "I don't see anything I like here."

Arif shrugged at Nizan, as if to apologize. "My brother's wife," he said. "She has very particular tastes."

"Of course," Nizan said, his face not betraying a hint of disappointment as he bowed them out.

"Nothing," Sammi said, once they were out in the street once more.

"Are you certain?"

"Of course not. I don't even know what I'm looking for. But whatever it is, I didn't see it."

Arif looked at his wristwatch, a Patek Philippe boasting separate dials for the times in various cities around the world. In Marrakesh, the afternoon was waning, something Sammi hardly needed an expensive watch to tell her. "Maybe we should split up," Arif said. "It will be faster. You do three, I do three."

"All right. Point me in the right direction."

Arif pulled out a map and showed her three locations on it.

As he did so, Naeem and his cohort appeared behind them in the doorway of Nizan's shop. Amun joined them a moment later. The three of them watched as Arif headed off to the east, Sammi to the northwest.

"Follow the woman," Amun ordered. "She will lead us to Gabriel Hunt."

17

DARIF DROVE GABRIEL AND LUCY THE THIRTY MILES
to Menara International. It was a long drive, made
longer by an overturned truck that snarled traffic
in both directions on the N8 highway—but at least
this time they got to ride in the cab rather than in
the trailer. Gabriel even managed a brief catnap on
the way.

Lucy accepted Darif's profuse farewells and
followed Gabriel to the airport's courtesy desk, where
a young woman nodded sympathetically while Gabriel
explained the situation. She turned the heavy black-
painted telephone on the counter around to face him
and he lost no time in putting a collect call through to
New York.

"Let's get you a ride back home," he said to Lucy
while he waited for Michael to answer.

"Do you really think it's safe for me to go back to
Nice?"

"No, of course not," Gabriel said. "I mean *home* home. New York."

"New York? Gabriel, I'm not—"

Michael picked up at that moment. "Michael," Gabriel said. "Guess who I found."

"I'm not going to New York!"

Michael's voice sounded shallow and tinny through the ancient phone equipment. "Gabriel?" he said. "Is that—"

But he got no further, since Lucy reached over and depressed the button in the handset cradle to disconnect the call.

"Now, is that any way to treat your brother?" Gabriel said. "Either of your brothers?"

"I am *not* going to New York," she said.

"Well, you're not staying here."

"No, and I'm not going back to Nice," Lucy said. "Aren't we fortunate that there are more than three cities in the world?"

"What's wrong with New York? You could stay at the Foundation. The security there is top-notch. Michael would love to take care of you, make sure nothing bad happens."

"That," Lucy said, "is what's wrong with New York." She shook her head. "I'm sorry, Gabriel. But I'm just not ready to see him again."

"It's been nine years," Gabriel said. "When are you going to be ready?"

"Give me another nine," Lucy said, "and we'll talk."

Gabriel threw his hands up. "So where do you want to go?"

"I'll go to Paris. Or back to Arezzo. Or, hell, I can crash with Devrim in Istanbul—"

"I don't know."

"Look. Paris is a big place. They won't find me there. I'll disappear. I've done it before. I'll send you e-mail and you can let me know when it's safe to go back to Nice. Meanwhile maybe I can turn Sammi up, find out what's happened to her."

"In Paris?"

"It's where she'd go if she couldn't stay in Nice."

Assuming she's even alive, Gabriel thought.

"All right," he said. "Paris—but you promise you'll stay out of sight? You won't contact anyone but me or Michael? Just till this thing is over."

"Don't worry about me," Lucy said. "You just worry about yourself. You don't need any more scars."

"You're telling me," Gabriel said, and reached out a knuckle to brush her chin.

He picked up the phone again, waited for the operator to come on the line. "Collect call," he said. "Same number as before."

"I THINK WE GOT DISCONNECTED," GABRIEL SAID. "THE phones in this part of the world—"

"You knew," Michael said. "That she was Cifer."

Gabriel started to say something and then stopped, the words dying in his throat. Lucy was watching him. He wondered if she could hear what Michael was saying.

"Yes, I knew," Gabriel said.

"Why did you lie to me? You told me Cifer was a six-foot-tall man with tattoos."

"That was true, about the tattoos."

"I suppose that's something," Michael said. He didn't sound angry—just hurt.

"She didn't want you to know, Michael. She was entitled to her privacy."

"Why does she hate me?"

Gabriel saw Lucy wince. He covered the mouthpiece of the phone. "Why don't you give us a moment," he said. "Maybe get some food."

"No money, remember?" But she headed off in the direction of the airport's restaurant anyway. Before she reached it she turned aside and pushed open the door of the bathroom.

Gabriel got back on the phone. "She doesn't hate you, Michael. She just doesn't want to see you."

"Why?"

"Says she's not ready yet," Gabriel said.

"She was ready to see you, apparently," Michael said.

"Three times in nine years," Gabriel said. "For maybe an hour apiece."

"That's three hours more than she gave me."

"I'm sorry, Michael. I know how you feel."

"Do you?"

"I never heard from her at all until last year, in Istanbul. You at least got e-mails."

"Under a fake name!"

"Yeah, well. I guess we've both got something to complain about. Right now, though, what matters is that she's alive, and out of the hands of the Alliance. And if we want to keep her that way, we need to get her to Paris."

"To Paris," Michael said.

"That's right. And me to Corsica."

"Corsica!" Michael said.

"Yes, Corsica. And Paris."

"She's not willing to come to New York," Michael said.

"You heard her," Gabriel said.

"I certainly did," Michael said. "Right before she hung up on me. She did hang up, right?" Gabriel said nothing. "Fine. I'll book her on a commercial flight; you can take the jet to Corsica."

"How long will it take Charlie to get to Marrakesh?" Gabriel said.

"Hardly any time at all, given that he's already there."

"He is?"

"Sure," Michael said. "I got a call from your friend Samantha saying you were in trouble and she needed to follow you to Marrakesh. How do you think I found out about 'Cifer'?"

A call from your friend Samantha—

"She's alive?"

"She was a few hours ago."

"So where is she?"

"Looking for you. I put her in touch with Reza Arif."

"Arif!" Gabriel said. "Why him?"

"She needed *someone* to help her," Michael said. "I admit he may not be the most trustworthy person we've ever—"

"The *most* trustworthy? No, I wouldn't say you could describe him as the most trustworthy. Just like you couldn't describe Taft as the skinniest president."

"I did warn her about him," Michael said.

At the other end of the terminal, the bathroom door opened and Lucy stepped out. "Listen I've got to go. Just get Lucy on the next flight to Paris. We'll talk about the rest later." He hung up on Michael's protests and joggled the button in the cradle to bring the operator back on the line. He gave her Sammi's cell phone number, waited while it rang twice.

Lucy, Gabriel saw, was slowly making her way back to the counter.

"Allo?"

"Sammi?" he said, keeping his voice low. "It's Gabriel."

"Gabriel! My God, where are you?"

"At the Marrakesh airport. Where are you?"

"In the city, at the Djemaa el Fna."

"Is Reza with you?"

"No—we split up to cover more ground."

"Good. How quickly can you meet me here?"

"Without him? I can't. He's got the car keys."

"Keys?" Gabriel said. "I've seen the way you drive. Don't tell me you don't know how to hotwire a car."

"Of course I know how to hotwire a car. But I shouldn't just leave him—"

"Do it," Gabriel said—and hung up just as Lucy reached the counter.

"Who was that," she said, "that you were telling to hotwire a car?"

If she knew Sammi was here…

If she knew, she'd never take the plane to Paris. She'd insist on staying, and she'd remain in danger.

"A man Michael put me in touch with," Gabriel said. "Someone he thought might be able to help out. You feeling better?"

"I peed, if that's what you mean," Lucy said. "So what's the verdict? Michael willing to fly me to Paris, or does he insist on a detour through New York first?"

"He doesn't like it," Gabriel said, "but he's willing." He turned the phone around and pushed it back toward the woman behind the counter. "Come on."

NAEEM PLACED A CALL TO AMUN AFTER HE AND Thabit had followed Sammi and her stolen car onto the expressway.

"She's in a blue Citroen," Naeem said. "On her way to the airport."

"Then that is where Hunt is," Amun answered. "And his sister. I will alert our men at the airport. Meanwhile—do not let the French woman out of your sight."

"Of course," Naeem said.

LUCY LOOKED AT THE BANK OF CLOCKS HIGH UP ON the terminal wall. "I should go. They'll be boarding soon."

Gabriel nodded. Just as well—Sammi would arrive in a few minutes, and he wanted Lucy safely out of the way before she did. "All right."

Gabriel pulled her into his arms and hugged her hard. "I'll e-mail you," she said.

"The person you really should e-mail is Michael," Gabriel said. "Or better yet, call him. Let him know you're safe."

She pulled herself out of his grip and walked down the corridor toward the security checkpoint. She got in line and called back to him. "Gabriel?"

"Yes?"

"I'll think about it."

He nodded, turned, and left.

THE LINE HAD BARELY MOVED AT ALL WHEN AN AIRPORT official wearing a Customs uniform approached Lucy.

"Could you please come with me, miss?"

"What?"

"Please come with me."

"Why? I'm waiting to go through security. My flight is in twenty minutes. They're probably boarding already."

"I'm sorry, you must come with me to Customs."

"But why?"

"Are you resisting arrest, madam?"

"*Arrest?* For what?"

The man lowered his voice and took her arm. "Come with me. Now." She felt a gun poke into her side. He held it close to his body, unseen by anyone else. "Come quietly," the man said, "or you die right here."

She looked around, gauged her chances if she made a break for it, or if she fought. She saw the man's head shake minutely from side to side and felt the gun's barrel press more deeply into her flesh. She swallowed. "All right."

The agent led her away and through a door marked AUTHORIZED PERSONNEL ONLY in English, Arabic, and French. Waiting for them in a small office was a stranger, a swarthy man in a neatly tailored suit.

"Miss Hunt," he said as the customs agent roughly twisted her arms behind her back and handcuffed her. "I regret that we meet under these unfortunate circumstances. I know your brothers and have all the respect in the world for them. True gentlemen, both of them."

"But then—why…?"

"Khufu was very upset that you left without saying goodbye. I'm afraid he insists you return."

"Who *are* you?" Lucy said. "Why are you working for them?"

"Why? Because they pay me," the man said. "As for who I am…" He bowed slightly from the waist. "Reza Arif, at your service."

* * *

SAMMI DOUBLE-PARKED THE HOTWIRED CITROEN outside the Baggage Claim area and ran inside. She found Gabriel more or less in the same spot she'd met Arif. He swept her up in his arms and she found hers going around his neck. She hadn't planned to kiss him; she got the sense it surprised them both when she did. But neither of them seemed in any hurry to end it.

"I was so worried about you," she said when they finally separated. "Are you all right?"

"I've been worse," he said. "You?"

She looked away. *If anyone could understand—*

"I killed two men," she said.

"Did you," Gabriel said, and stroked her hair gently. "Well. I'm sure they had it coming."

"One did," she said.

"I'm sorry," he said.

"It was terrible," she said. "I did not know if you were alive or dead; I did not know if would live or die, I just knew I had to—had to…"

He took her in his arms again. "It's okay." Then he whispered something into her ear. "When I say 'duck'…"

"What?"

"*Duck!*" he shouted, and pressed one palm down on the top of her head while drawing his Colt with the other. Sammi dropped and rolled toward the metal bench against the nearest wall, wedging herself beneath it. She saw Gabriel running toward a pair of open glass doors, where two men with guns were charging toward him. All three guns were roaring and spitting flame; airline staff and deplaning passengers were running, screaming, trying to get out of the way.

One of the men went down, sprawling as the impact of a bullet above his right knee swept his legs out from under him. The other one kept coming, squeezing off shot after shot in Gabriel's direction. Gabriel hunched down and a glass light fixture just past his shoulder exploded into fragments.

He whipped up a suitcase in one hand, saying "Sorry" to the astonished tourist who'd been reaching down to pick it up, and hurled it at the remaining gunman. The heavy bag split open in midair, punctured by a pair of gunshots, scattering clothing and duty free souvenirs in all directions; but the bullets didn't halt the bag's momentum and it smashed into the shooter's hand with an audible crack. The gun flew out of the man's hand and he dropped to his knees, cursing and cradled his broken wrist.

Gabriel ran back to the bench and extended a hand. Sammi grabbed hold and pulled herself to her feet. "Come on," he said and raced toward a door marked "PRIVATE FLIGHTS." They shot through and Gabriel slammed the door shut behind them, twisting the lock.

"Can I help you?" a young woman asked. She was well trained—her voice exuded calm and professionalism in spite of the sounds of gunfire she must have heard coming through the door.

"Yes," Gabriel said. "Hunt Foundation, Gabriel Hunt. Where's our plane?"

They heard someone try the doorknob, then start hammering on the door.

"Do you have any ID?" the woman said.

Gabriel grinned ruefully. He waved his Colt at her. "Honey, this is all the ID I've got, and it's going to have to be good enough."

A huge blow rocked the door. It wouldn't stand up to many more.

"I'm sorry, sir," the woman said, "but I am going to have to confirm with the pilot…"

"Come on, we'll go confirm together." Gabriel pushed past her, past the counter, and kicked open the metal door behind her. Across a hundred feet of sun-baked tarmac, the Hunt Foundation jet sat with its cockpit door open and stairs extended. A man in short sleeves sat at the top of the stairs, reading an issue of *Plane and Pilot*.

"Charlie!" Gabriel yelled as he ran toward the plane. "Get off your ass and get the engine started!"

Behind them, Sammi heard the door lock splinter.

"Sir," the woman called breathlessly. She was running behind them, as fast as she could. "This man claims he's Gabriel Hunt. Can you confirm—"

"That's Gabriel, all right," Charlie called back, and he disappeared into the cockpit.

"Happy?" Gabriel said.

The woman stopped running; she stood bent over, her hands on her knees, panting. Sammi knew how she felt. But she kept pushing till they reached the foot of the stairs, then followed Gabriel up, taking the steps two at a time. The stairs began retracting the instant her feet cleared the last step.

Looking out the window, she saw three men—two in airport uniforms, one in plainclothes—race across the tarmac after them. But Charlie already had the plane taxiing. A few gunshots sounded dully and one bullet spanged off the side of the plane. Then their nose was up and the ground dropped away behind them.

"Where we going?" Charlie called from the cockpit.

"Corsica," Gabriel called back.

PRESSING HIS HAND AGAINST THABIT'S LEG WOUND, Naeem made another call to Amun.

"They got away," he reported. "On a private jet."

"Never mind," Amun said. "He will go right where we want him to, and he won't raise a finger against us. Not now that we have his sister again."

18

GABRIEL WAS GLAD FOR THE CHANCE TO TAKE A proper shower and change his clothes. He apologized to Sammi for not having anything on board she could change into.

"That's all right," she said, tousling his wet hair. "I'll make do." She shut the door between them. Gabriel heard the sound of the shower's spray going on, then a zipper sliding down and a pair of shoes being kicked off. Then he heard the spray interrupted as she got in, followed by a low growl of contentment.

She'd be a while. Gabriel went up front to talk with Charlie.

"All due respect, Mister Hunt," Charlie said, "you can't just come running and expect me to take off on a dime. Not at a busy airport. Took a miracle to make it out of there without hitting anything."

It was the longest speech Gabriel had ever heard from the man. He patted Charlie's shoulder. "Didn't take a miracle, just a great pilot."

Charlie grumbled. But it was true—he'd seen Gabriel out of many a tight spot.

"Still," he said. "Your brother wouldn't like you taking risks like that. Or me, with Foundation property."

"He ever complains to you about it," Gabriel said, "you just tell him to talk to me."

He sat in the co-pilot's seat for the next hundred miles, watching Africa's northwest coast disappear behind them and the south of Spain come into view. In the distance he could just make out the small humps in the water that were the Balearic Islands.

He thought about the ordeal Lucy had been through, and the one Sammi had. At least Lucy was on her way to Paris—that was one less thing to worry about, a big one. But Sammi was with him now, and he knew there was no way she'd agree to stay behind with the plane when they landed. He could tell her that Lucy had gone to Paris and would be looking for her there, encourage her to let Charlie fly her there, too—but he had a feeling she wasn't going to let him face the Alliance on his own in Corsica any more than she had in Cairo. And the truth was it might be good to have her along. She was the historian, after all, not him, and her store of knowledge about Napoleon seemed likely to be more than a little useful if he wanted to get his hands on the Second Stone.

From the main cabin he heard the sound of the bathroom door opening, then footsteps padding toward the rear of the plane and storage compartments opening, one after another. When Gabriel went back, he saw Sammi standing with a blanket clutched around her, the fabric bunched in one fist.

"You really *don't* have anything a girl could wear,"

she said, and swung the compartment door shut. "Not even a spare stewardess uniform."

"No stewardesses," Gabriel said, coming toward her.

"Oh? What do you do if you get thirsty in the middle of a flight?"

"I go to the galley," Gabriel said, "and forage for myself."

"And if you get lonely," she said, "in the middle of a flight? Do you take care of that for yourself, too?"

He stopped an arm's length from her and looked her up and down, from her bare feet to her dripping auburn hair. "Miss Ficatier, if I didn't know better, I'd think you were offering me an alternative."

She smiled at him. "Who says you know better?"

WHEN SHE WOKE, PLEASANTLY SORE AND IN NEED OF another shower, Sammi saw Gabriel over by one of the windows, sketching on a piece of paper. She went over.

Gabriel looked up. "Your clothes are probably dry by now." After her shower, she'd rinsed them in the bathroom sink and hung them on the towel rod.

"I'll put them on in a bit," she said. "Unless you mind—"

"Not in the slightest," Gabriel said, kissing the side of her breast, "and Charlie's too much of a gentleman to peek."

Sammi stretched, heard her shoulders crack. "What are you working on?"

"A map," Gabriel said. "Doing my best to reconstruct it from memory. Amun had it in his office—"

"Amun!" Sammi exclaimed, snapping her fingers. "I *knew* there was something I needed to tell you. I know who he is!"

"So do I," Gabriel said. "He's the second-in-command of the Alliance of the Pharaohs."

"Maybe—but he's also the professor I was telling you about, the one who taught the Mediterranean History course we took. Omar Amun. Did you get my text message?"

"Your text...?"

Then Gabriel remembered. Back in Cairo.

THAT'S THE PRO

That's the professor.

"I got part of it," Gabriel said.

"Well, they grabbed me while I was typing it," Sammi said. "I wasn't sure I even pressed 'Send.' "

"What the hell is a history professor from Nice doing high up in an organization like the Alliance?"

"I don't know," Sammi said. "He was just a visiting professor... and he did talk a lot about 'Egypt for the Egyptians' and so forth, but..."

"But you didn't think he'd cut anyone's head off over it."

"No," Sammi said. Her face fell. "I feel... I feel terrible about the whole thing. I was the one who talked Cifer into taking his class—and I was the one who told him about you."

Gabriel frowned. "What do you mean, told him about me?"

"There were only thirty seats in the class, and more than a hundred people applying. I thought it would help, that Cifer was the sister of the famous explorer, Gabriel Hunt..."

"I'm sure it did," Gabriel said. "Especially once he realized he could get me to do the Alliance's bidding by kidnapping her."

"I didn't know he would—" Sammi began, but

Gabriel pressed a finger against her lips.

"You couldn't have known," he said. "It's not your fault."

"Except that it is. And now she is god only knows where, suffering god only knows what—"

"Sh," Gabriel said. "Lucy's fine."

"What?"

"I got her out. She's on a plane to Paris right now."

"She's…? Really?" Sammi's voice betrayed her excitement and relief. "You wouldn't say that just to make me feel better—"

"Of course not," Gabriel said. "Lucy's fine."

Sammi was startled to feel tears running down her cheeks. Gabriel drew her to his chest and she buried her face in his shirt. "I was so worried—so worried…"

He put his pen down and stroked the back of her head.

After a moment she looked up. "But if she really is fine," she said, "and on her way back to France… why did you tell Charlie to take us to Corsica?"

"Let me tell you a story," Gabriel said.

CHARLIE TOUCHED DOWN SMOOTHLY AT CAMPO dell'Oro Airport, located on the east side of the Gulf of Ajaccio, just north of the mouth of the Gravona River. The capital of Corsica sat on the western side of the island, a little south of the halfway median that bisected the country. It was the largest and most modern city in Corsica, though that wasn't saying much—none of the municipalities were particularly large, and most were simple villages. Ajaccio had perhaps fifty thousand inhabitants. Among its few claims to fame was that it was the birthplace of Napoleon Bonaparte.

In the airport Gabriel tore a map from a pad of them at the car rental counter and compared it to the one he'd sketched out on the plane. He'd marked as many of the pinned landmarks as he could recall, particularly the ones near the spot where "the web" had been written in Arabic. It was an area in Southern Corsica near Filitosa, in the rough wilderness that Corsicans called the "maquis." The last time he'd been to Corsica, Gabriel had gone to that region, pursuing a legendary urn rumored to have been buried beneath one of the clusters of menhirs—large, upright standing stones that had been carved around 1,500 B.C. The urn had turned out to be a myth, but Gabriel's photographs of the strange and paganistic menhirs had been good for a feature article in *National Geographic*.

If Napoleon had wanted to keep the Second Stone hidden, Gabriel thought, he couldn't have chosen a better place for it—doubly so if he'd believed the stone to have mystical properties. Growing up in Corsica, he must have heard every fable and legend about the strange powers of this territory, and the endless maze of caves and rock structures buried in the hills certainly offered no shortage of hiding places.

With his money belt refilled from the stash on board the plane and a new Hunt Foundation credit card in his pocket, Gabriel had no difficulty renting a Renault Laguna 1.8 at the airport. He and Sammi drove it into the city and spent an hour and a half at a hardware store buying supplies: water and food, rope, climbing tools, flashlights, pickaxes. The final expenditure, because it was dark by the time they got out, was a hotel room for the night. At the front desk, Gabriel found himself confronted by the baleful eye of the manager, whose glance flicked from Gabriel to Sammi, from their naked ring fingers to their ankles, where no luggage stood. "Is Monsieur certain he wishes but a single room, and not two? I can offer a most reasonable price on a second…"

Sammi stepped forward and matched the man glare for glare. "Monsieur is certain," she said coldly in French, "and so is madame. One room will do, and I suggest you make it one without neighbors on either side if your guests are as sensitive about these things as you."

The man handed over a key glacially. "Very well," he said.

But in the end, the only noise they made in the room would have been inoffensive had their neighbors been librarians on one side and nuns on the other. A room service dinner of sadly overcooked steak and undercooked vegetables was followed by a phone call back to New York, where it was two in the morning but Michael nevertheless answered on the first ring.

"Have you heard from Lucy?" he wanted to know.

"I wouldn't know," Gabriel said. "I don't have e-mail, and my phone's…"

"You phone is what?" Michael asked.

"Not so much a phone anymore as a collection of phone pieces. Lying somewhere in Cairo."

Michael was silent for a moment, no doubt mourning the $30,000 piece of equipment. But only for a moment—his primary concern lay elsewhere. "If she couldn't get you, she'd at least have called me, don't you think?"

"I asked her to," Gabriel said. "She didn't make any promises."

"Her plane landed hours ago," Michael said.

"I'm sure she's fine," Gabriel said. "If you want to

worry about something, let me give you something else to chew on."

Gabriel gave him Amun's name and a quick summary of what Sammi had said about him. "I'll have someone check him out," Michael said. "See what I can find out. But Gabriel…"

"Yes?"

"I'm going to try to find Lucy first. I know she doesn't want to talk to me—and she doesn't have to. But I need to know she's okay. I have a bad feeling somehow."

"You have a bad feeling about everything," Gabriel said.

"And how often have I been right?"

"Not more than ninety-eight percent of the time," Gabriel said.

Sammi came over as he was hanging up the phone. "Something wrong?"

"He's worried about Lucy because she hasn't called."

"Well, don't you think—"

"Sammi," Gabriel said, "she hasn't called him in nine years. She's fine." Silently he added, *And if she's not, we're on the trail of the one thing that might help.*

"THEY WENT TO A HOTEL," NAEEM REPORTED OVER his cell phone. "I can get the room number from the clerk, enter while they're sleeping…"

"No," Amun answered. "Do nothing of the sort. Do you understand? I am on my way. Just watch them— that is all. Do not touch them, do not speak to them. We need them alive."

"You need Hunt," Naeem protested, "and his sister. But the French woman…?"

"Are you questioning me?" Amun said.

"Of course not," Naeem said.

"Good," Amun said. "Now do your job."

Naeem tried to keep the frustration out of his voice. "Understood."

THEY CHECKED OUT OF THE HOTEL AT DAWN.

Corsica was a beautiful country, in a rough-hewn way. There was nothing soft about it. Mountainous throughout much of its middle, it was a country as rugged as any Gabriel had been to and not only physically. Although technically part of France, Corsica was more Italian in culture and sensibility, and its people had a quality all their own, strong and unsentimental, almost brutal. The word "vendetta" originated in Corsica, and the *Union Corse*—the Corsican mafia—had been a powerful force in daily life on the island for most of the past century. Even now, officially crushed, it still had its tentacles in businesses throughout the country. Corsicans were hard people, living in a hard environment.

Gabriel drove south toward Propriano and the small community of Sollacaro, which hosted the Filitosa site. If there was something to be found, this was where they had to start looking.

"THEY ARE HEADED TOWARD THE SITE," NAEEM reported.

"Excellent," Amun said. "You know what to do if he makes it inside the Web."

"What about the Corsicans who guard it?"

"Kemnebi will take care of them. He is assembling a team. If it proves necessary, we will intervene."

"Understood," Naeem said. Then after Amun had disconnected and the cell phone was safely closed, he said contemptuously, "*If* it proves necessary."

THEY REACHED FILITOSA BY MID-MORNING. IT WAS IN the middle of a dense forest that seemed to be untouched by modern civilization. Gabriel parked the car, took the pair of rucksacks they'd filled with their gear, and handed one to Sammi, who shrugged it on. Together they went into the Repository Museum building, where visitors bought tickets to visit the site. The museum contained a number of specimens excavated from various archaeological digs on the property. Glass display cases held artifacts such as obsidian arrowheads and pottery from the late Neolithic period. Gabriel led Sammi past the ranks of cases and straight to the outside path that led through an ancient olive grove to the first monument. Walking down the hill from there, they came to the monument, which consisted of menhirs with crudely carved faces erected around an open-air shrine. A number of hut platforms also surrounded the area.

Gabriel studied the map he had drawn. "We need to go to the very bottom of the hill, where the Western Monument and *torri* are located."

"What's a *torri*?"

"A type of circular stone structure. It's thought they were used as temples. Come on."

They continued along the path. Menhirs were arranged in a ritualistic circle near walls of stone that had once enclosed—what? No one knew. Gabriel had asked Michael once. It was obvious that the ancient Corsicans had used the structure for religious purposes, but historians weren't sure what that religion was.

Beyond the monument was a fence—the end of the Filitosa property.

"We have to get over that fence without being seen," Gabriel said. There weren't too many people around—it was still early. They walked to a section of the fence partly concealed behind a stand of large olive trees.

"Okay, quick." Gabriel held his hands together to give Sammi a boost. She placed a foot in his palm, caught hold of the top of the fence with both hands and nimbly hoisted herself up. In an instant she was down on the other side and had disappeared into the thick foliage. Gabriel was reminded of the way she'd vanished from Lucy's apartment in Nice.

"Coming?" came an impatient whisper.

Gabriel took a look around to make sure no one had come into view, then pulled himself up to the top of the fence. Before he could put his leg over, he heard a telephone ringing somewhere beneath him—Sammi's cell phone.

He vaulted over the top of the fence and dropped into the undergrowth, where Sammi was fumbling in her pocket. The phone rang again. Gabriel hissed, *"Turn that thing—"*

She flipped it open and answered in a whisper. *"Oui?"* She listened for a moment. "Yes, he is right here." She handed the phone to Gabriel. "It is your brother. He says it is urgent."

Gabriel took the phone. "Michael, once again, not a good time."

"I was right, Gabriel," Michael said, miserably. "She's been kidnapped again."

"What?"

"I said Lucy's been—"

"How did it happen? In Paris?"

"No. She never made it on the plane."

Gabriel's hand tightened around the phone. "Damn it."

"I just got another e-mail from the Alliance. It says you have to 'deliver the Stone to us or your sister will die.'"

"They must know we're here," Gabriel said.

"You want me to call the police?" Michael said. "Interpol?"

"No. They'd be useless—or worse. These people are not amateurs. They'll kill her if we give them a reason."

"So what are you going to do?"

"Get their goddamn stone for them." He hung up. The look on Sammi's face told him he didn't need to relay the news. "Don't worry," Gabriel said, "we'll get her back."

"What if we can't?"

Gabriel didn't answer. He just took another look at his map, jammed it in his pocket, and headed toward a thick crop of trees.

THE TRACK LED THEM DEEPER INTO THE DARK FOREST. Sunlight barely filtered through the tops of the tall pine trees. Twenty minutes of climbing over knotted roots and fallen and rotting tree trunks brought them to a small clearing that began where they were standing and ended a dozen feet away, at a wall of boulders. It was as tall as a three-story building, as wide as four buses driving bumper-to-bumper.

"Is this a natural formation?" Sammi asked, looking at the giant, irregular stones. "Or was there a rock slide...?"

"Neither," Gabriel said. "I think they were put here. Like the menhirs."

"But these are enormous," she said. "How could they even have moved them, never mind lifted them...?"

"Nobody knows," Gabriel said. "But here they are. And the map says we need to be on the other side."

"I don't see a way around," Sammi said.

"There isn't one," Gabriel said. He was already undoing the closure of his rucksack and gestured to Sammi to do the same. "We're going to have to go over."

He took out a length of rope and tied one end to her waist, then fastened the other to his own. "I'll go first. Just follow my lead. Place your feet exactly where I put mine. All right?"

She leaned in and kissed him, just briefly. "For luck," she said.

"Let's hope we don't need it," he said.

Gabriel shimmied up the first boulder, found a foothold, and then struck the pickaxe into the rock above him. That gave him something to grab. He hammered a spring-loaded camming device into the crack between two big rocks and quickly attached a carabiner to it, then secured the rope. Using this anchor, he was able to climb to a higher rock, repeat the procedure, and move on. When he was four boulders up, he called for Sammi to follow. She bounded up the first rock like a pro, carefully mimicked Gabriel's footwork, and scurried onto the second. They were on their way.

It took them a little over forty minutes to reach the top of the boulders. "That wasn't so bad," Sammi said.

"We're not done," Gabriel said. "Now we go down."

They reversed the process. Down generally took less time than up, but was more dangerous. When ascending during a rock climb, you can see what's ahead. When you're going down, you can't.

"Take it slow," Gabriel said. "Pay attention to every step. It just takes one—" Gabriel felt some loose pebbles slip beneath his sole and leaned in toward the rock face to regain his balance.

"Are you okay?'

"As I was saying," Gabriel said.

They went the rest of the way slowly, cautiously, Gabriel wondering with every step whether Amun or Kemnebi or another of Khufu's minions was watching them at this very moment, from the branches of a nearby tree or through the high-powered scope of a sniper rifle.

Sammi dropped to the ground beside him, a little out of breath. "How did I do?"

"You're a natural." Gabriel quickly packed the climbing tools and took out his handmade map. "Here is where it gets complicated. I'm not sure where we're supposed to go next. Neither was the Alliance. The place we're looking for—" he pointed to the area labeled in Arabic "—is somewhere around here, but exactly where... I don't know." He looked at the thick wall of trees directly ahead of them. "You'd think there would be a marker of some kind."

"After two hundred years?"

"There's apparently a group still in existence that's devoted to keeping the secret."

"Then wouldn't they want to get rid of any markers?"

"Not if the markers are part of the secret they're protecting," Gabriel said.

Sammi studied the terrain in front of her. "Is this what you Americans mean when you say 'can't see the forest for the trees'?"

"Might as well be." Gabriel began to walk along the tree line, studying the ground and the trunks. He found no signs of recent visitation, nor any indication of any man-made objects. He looked at the map again. "I don't get it. It's as if the trail stops cold."

"Are you sure it really exists?"

He thought of the nonexistent urn he'd come to Corsica to find the last time. "I'm beginning to wonder."

He put the map away and moved forward, through the trees. There was no trail, so the brush was difficult to step across. Sammi tailed behind him.

"Watch your step," he warned.

As they continued deeper into the *maquis,* Gabriel systematically scanned their surroundings left and right. If they didn't find something concrete soon, they'd have to turn back. What consequences that might have for Lucy, he didn't know and didn't want to contemplate. He could tell the Alliance that in his expert opinion the Stone didn't exist, or at least the hiding place on Corsica didn't. They might even believe him—but that wouldn't stop them from killing him. Or Lucy.

Maybe if he could break her free again, get her back to New York—

He never had the chance to finish the thought, because at that moment he saw the menhir.

It was twenty yards in front of them and off to one side, hidden by an especially dense group of trees, a menhir similar to the ones behind them at Filitosa. Gabriel ran toward it, Sammi at his heels. He pushed aside a branch and stepped closer. This one wasn't ancient. It was old—but not prehistoric. The stone wasn't nearly as weathered, the features on the carved face at the top more distinct.

It was the face of a young man—a boy, really—and on the sides of the towering stone were the suggestions of a military uniform. The figure's face was turned to the left, in profile.

"I don't believe it," Sammi said.

"What?"

She pointed up toward where the figure's shoulders would have been if it were a full sculpture. "The insignia of the Military College of Brienne. He was not yet ten years old. This is Napoleon, Gabriel."

"Are you sure?"

She nodded. "It was when he first left Corsica. He came back during the Revolution, and once later, after returning from Egypt—but he was never again to make his home here for any length of time. This was the last age at which he was purely a Corsican—when he was still Napoleone di Buonaparte, not yet Napoléon Bonaparte."

Gabriel walked around the menhir. "That tells us the trail exists. The question is, where do we go from here?"

Sammi followed the statue's gaze to the left. "Maybe this way?"

"Makes as much sense as anything."

They walked through the brush in that direction. A hollow log, the remnant of a fallen tree, lay across their path. Gabriel stepped over it, but as he set his foot down, something snapped.

"Don't move," Gabriel said.

Sammi looked around. "What is it?"

Gabriel was studying the log and the ground around it. He picked up a thin cord that had been attached to a spring mechanism. "It was booby-trapped."

"But nothing happened," Sammi said.

Gabriel shook his head. "Nothing we can see," he

said. He let the cord drop. "It triggered something. Probably an alarm."

"I don't hear anything."

"Neither do I. Yet." He drew his Colt.

They continued on in as close to a straight line as they could, through another thick grove of trees. On the far side, a narrow path opened up. Gabriel hurried along it until it widened into a clearing, roughly the same size as the one beside the wall of boulders. Only here there were no boulders, no wall—just a grassy slope, and in the side of the slope, an opening loosely concealed behind dead tree branches.

"Sammi, I think we may have found it," Gabriel said. He heard something behind him, something heavy thudding to the ground. "Sammi?"

He spun around.

Silently and out of nowhere, six armed men had appeared between the trees. They all had guns—rifles and pistols—pointed at Gabriel. Sammi was lying face down at the feet of a seventh man who held the butt of his rifle angled above the back of her head.

Gabriel let his gun fall to the ground and slowly raised his hands. The man standing over Sammi, his broad Corsican features ruddy, had dark eyes, grey-black hair, and a full beard. He stepped forward.

"You are trespassing," he said. "You may not go farther. In fact, you will not leave this place alive."

19

"WE'RE NOT YOUR ENEMY," GABRIEL SAID.

"Any man who sets foot here is my enemy," the man said.

"There is a group in Egypt, the Alliance of the Pharaohs—*Alliance Pharaonique*. They've taken your men in the past, tortured them. And now they've kidnapped my sister. Said they would kill her if I didn't find the Second Stone for them."

The man didn't budge. "Then I am very sorry for you. It is a terrible thing to lose a sister. But at least you will have the comfort of dying first."

"Hang on," Gabriel said, "nobody has to die. We all want the same thing—the group in Egypt stopped. Surely there's a way to—"

At the man's feet, Sammi groaned.

"Can I help her up?" Gabriel said. When the man didn't respond, Gabriel added, "You can shoot us if you want. But until you do, I'm going to help her."

"Is she armed?"

"No."

The man nodded slightly. Gabriel bent and extended a hand to Sammi, and she pulled herself up. She was unsteady on her feet and she winced when she put a hand to the back of her skull.

"Who are you?" she said.

The men said nothing.

"They're the group organized by Napoleon's brother," Gabriel said. "To protect the Second Stone. Am I right?"

"You are," the leader said, "and it is the seal on your death warrant. You know too much to live." He raised his rifle, and the men behind him followed suit.

Gabriel gauged the distance to his Colt. He couldn't outrun seven bullets.

"Wait," he said. "I have a proposition—"

"What proposition?" the man said.

Gabriel's mind was racing, trying to come up with an answer to that question. He saw the man's finger tighten on the trigger and began blurting out the first thing that came to mind, "We could make a—"

But Gabriel's words were drowned out by a barrage of gunfire. Gabriel and Sammi both flinched and looked down at their own chests, but no bullets had struck them. Looking up, they saw spots of crimson erupting across the leader's torso. His eyes rolled up into his head and he dropped to his knees, the rifle tumbling from his dead hands. The other men turned shouting in the direction the gunfire had come from and began firing blindly themselves.

Men wearing burnooses over their faces poured out of the forest, shooting as they came. Gabriel recognized the one in the lead—he didn't need to see Kemnebi's face to know it was him. Gabriel pulled Sammi to the ground as bullets whipped over their heads. The remaining Corsicans took cover behind trees. Skilled at maneuvering in this environment, they quickly vanished to obtain secure positions from which to shoot.

Gabriel's Colt lay a few feet away, next to the Corsican leader's body. Gabriel darted toward it but was forced back by a spray of bullets. "Gabriel!" Sammi shouted. Turning, he saw that one of the Egyptians had run out from the trees and into the clearing, unsheathing a long knife as he came. With his other hand, the man pulled his burnoose away from his face, revealing a bruised jaw—and eyes burning with rage. Sammi rolled out of his path just as his blade descended, a bitter declaration in Arabic spraying from his lips. Gabriel lunged for his pistol, grabbed it, and rolled onto his back, firing at the attacker in one fluid motion. The Colt's round slammed into the man's shoulder, causing him to stumble—but he kept coming, knife swinging wildly. Gabriel squeezed the trigger again, aiming dead center on the purple and yellow bruise on the man's face. The Colt jerked in his hand and the man went down, a spray of blood hanging in the air for an instant before pattering over his body.

Gabriel ran to Sammi in a crouch and pulled her toward the cave entrance.

Behind them, Gabriel heard the battle continuing fiercely, gunshots mixing with cries of pain, exclamations both in French and Arabic. The Corsican group may have been smaller in number, but they were managing to pick off the Alliance members. Gabriel glanced back and counted five bodies on the ground—besides the Corsican leader, the others were all Egyptian. It was what the Alliance got for attacking on the group's home turf. But Gabriel couldn't take much comfort from the fact, since if the Corsicans prevailed, it was what Gabriel and Sammi would get as well.

He started tearing away the loose branches covering the front of the cave, Sammi working beside him to open up enough room for them to squeeze inside. They got some help from a stray gunshot that splintered a particularly thick branch just inches away from Gabriel's hand. "Go," Gabriel said, pushing Sammi toward the narrow hole they'd opened, and she slipped in sideways. Gabriel stole another glance back. The gun battle was still raging; for the moment, no one had the luxury of paying attention to them. He squeezed into the cave after Sammi. The noise of gunfire was instantly muted, replaced by the echoing sound of Sammi panting in the darkness beside him.

"Is it safe here?" she asked.

Was it safe, she wanted to know.

It was *safer*, certainly—for now.

But Gabriel had a feeling they'd just walked into Napoleon's Web.

20

THE ENTRANCE THEY'D COME THROUGH WAS actually an abscess in the ground that narrowed to a tunnel through which only one person at a time could fit. Gabriel went first, with Sammi following directly behind him. He grabbed a flashlight from his rucksack and switched it on. The cave was dark, damp, and had a familiar smell of… yes, bat guano. "Watch your step," he said. "It's going to be slippery."

"All right."

"There are also supposed to be traps," Gabriel said.

"Traps?"

"Three of them. According to the Alliance's documents. Dreamed up by Napoleon himself and built to his specifications by his court engineer."

"You're not serious," Sammi said.

"They seemed to be."

He moved forward slowly. Where the flashlight's beam landed, he saw insects scurry away, and he could feel some crunching underfoot as well. The tunnel continued, branching and forking into a maze of twisty passages, all alike. Gabriel pressed forward, taking the rightmost fork each time, just to make it easier to backtrack if it proved necessary. And it did—twice they reached dead ends and had to retrace their steps.

But eventually they reached a larger, open space, obviously man-made, that was about the size of a large bedroom. It had been carved from the stone of the hillside, the walls and ceiling shored up with vaults of rock. The noise of their footsteps echoed loudly even after they came to a stop.

"Strange," Sammi said, and her voice reverberated: *strange... strange... strange...*

Gabriel heard a movement behind them, a swift scraping of stone against stone. He spun to face the entryway just in time to see it sealed up with a deafening thud as a stone slab slid into place from above. He ran up to it, searched along the base and sides for handholds, anything he might get a grip on and use to lift it. There weren't any—and even if there had been, the slab must have weighed half a ton at the least.

"My god," Sammi said, running up behind him, "did I do—" The echoes of her voice came back at her in a cacophonous crescendo, louder even than before they'd been sealed in, the repeated syllables crashing over one another. She covered her ears and let the end of her sentence remain unspoken.

Gabriel looked up as the echoes began to fade. He remembered another cave he'd been in, a cave of ice near the South Pole where the echoes of his party's voices had shaken loose a rain of stalactites, razor sharp and deadly to the touch. At least there were no stalactites here.

But there was also no vent to the outside, as far as he could tell, and therefore no source of air. If they couldn't find a way out of this room...

He clapped once and heard the concussive sound rebounding from wall to wall. Like being inside a drum.

"Look," Sammi said very quietly, and she pointed at the far wall as the room picked up her whispered word and threw it back at her: *look—look—look—look—look...*

Gabriel shined the light where Sammi was pointing. On the wall, chiseled into the rock, was an inscription in French:

Lui seul avec la voix et la qualité d'un français pourrait entrer.

The wall itself appeared to be constructed from several rectangular blocks of stone similar to the one that had sealed off the entryway. Beyond the blocks would be... another passage? *Only one with the voice and quality of a Frenchman may enter.* Enter—not exit. Clearly this was the way they had to go. Gabriel pressed against the stones with his shoulder. He couldn't budge them.

He leaned close to Sammi until his lips were pressed against her ear. "Any ideas?" he said in the tiniest voice he'd ever managed.

She shook her head.

Gabriel studied the stone wall more closely. He moved his fingers along the seam between the stones, tracing the outlines of each slab. There were no hidden levers or catches—not that he could find, anyway. There had to be another way to open it.

The voice of a Frenchman?

"*Bonjour,*" he said, with his mouth close to the wall.

And he heard something, a quiet scraping of metal deep inside the wall. He braced himself against the stone blocks again and shoved, hard, but nothing happened.

"Bonjour," he said again, more loudly, and heard the echoes of his voice career around him. Clearly, speaking was having an effect—but he had no idea what he needed to say. *"Vous êtes un tres jolie mur... ouvrez, s'il vous plait..."* He pushed against the stones as hard as he could, and though he could hear the internal mechanism moving within the wall, he might as well have been pushing against a mountain for all the good it did.

"You try," he said to Sammi, and she did, speaking in French while he continued pushing—but if anything the mechanism seemed to respond even less to her voice than to his.

"It reacts to sound," Gabriel said, having returned to Sammi's side. He spoke quietly, but didn't whisper. The danger now didn't seem to be that their voices would trigger a bad outcome; the danger was that they would fail to trigger a good one. "My voice more than yours, and—" He paused for a second. *"Français plus que l'Anglais."*

"French more than English," she said, and sure enough, the scratching of metal within the wall was less pronounced. "How is it possible? This was built when, in 1800?"

"Something like that."

"But it would require sophisticated technology—"

Gabriel shook his head. "Sounds are just vibrations—and each has its own distinct vibration. That's how record players work, right? The record vibrates the needle differently to produce each sound. Why couldn't someone in Napoleon's time have built a *reverse* record player, where each sound uttered makes a needle vibrate a bit differently? If the mechanism were sensitive enough…"

"But in 1800?" she said, forgetting to speak quietly. They waited for the echoes of her voice to die down. "They didn't even have record players then," she whispered.

"They had music boxes," Gabriel said. "And automata with bellows inside to make them sing. And wasn't de Martinville already working on the phonautograph in Paris?" Gabriel had been asked to find one of the Frenchman's original devices by the Louvre once—it consisted of a horn into which you spoke or sang and a cylinder turned by a crank that caused each sound that entered the horn to be uniquely transcribed by a stylus scratching against the wall of the cylinder…

"I think that was later," Sammi said, "more like 1850."

"Well, then someone else in France must have had the idea before him," Gabriel said, "since it seems to be what we're dealing with here."

He walked up to the wall and tried speaking the same word—*Ouvrez*—in different pitches and at different volumes. The lower his voice, the more the mechanism seemed to activate. But the movement remained purely internal—none of his attempts made the stones shift so much as an inch.

What had de Martinville's first phonautograph transcription been? A children's song. But which one? *Frere Jacques?* No. He remembered. "*Au clair de la lune,*" he sang, "*mon ami Pierrot…*"

This time the stones of the wall did shift slightly, rising a fraction of an inch off the ground, as if somewhere inside the wall a counterweight was being lowered.

"More!" Sammi said, and she joined in as well. But even their two voices combined, and redoubled by the echoes, were not enough to get the stones more than an inch off the ground. Gabriel thought of trying to get his fingers in under the stones—there was just about enough room. But that would be a good way to lose a couple of fingers, and a lousy way to get the passage open. Maybe if they had something in their rucksacks that could act as a crowbar or a lever…?

"That was better," Sammi said, when their voices had died down and the stone blocks had settled once more. "They moved."

"Not enough," Gabriel said.

"No, but I think singing was right—we just need to figure out the right song."

"And how are going to do that? There are thousands of French songs. How are we supposed to know which one was Napoleon's favor—" Gabriel fell silent, and the room fell silent a minute later.

"What is it?" Sammi said.

He answered her only with a confident smile. He put a finger to his lips, then cleared his throat and began to sing.

La victoire en chantant
Nous ouvre la barrière

Victory, singing, opens the barrier for us…

La Liberté guide nos pas
Ed du Nord au Midi

…Liberty guides our steps; and from North to South…

La trompette guerrière
A sonné l'heure des combats

The war trumpet has sounded the hour of battle.

With an enormous wrenching sound, the two central stones in the wall were hauled upwards, vanishing into the dark roof of the cavern. The stone blocking the entryway shot up as well, leaving them with a choice of exits.

But what sort of choice was it, really? Return to the scene of the gun battle empty handed?

And never know what lay beyond this room?

Gabriel gestured for Sammi to go through the opening while he continued to sing the *Chant du Départ*, Napoleon's hand-picked replacement for the *Marseillaise*. It hadn't caught on as the national anthem—but by god, he'd made it the anthem of his vault back on Corsica.

Gabriel eyed the stones warily as he passed under them, still singing, but they showed no sign of being about to come down again. Once he was on the other side, he stopped, and they stayed up—until, presumably, the next unfortunate soul came along and triggered the trap.

"How in the world do you come to know that song?" Sammi said. "I thought *I* was the historian."

"A good magician never reveals his secrets," Gabriel said, and led onward.

21

THE NEW TUNNEL THEY WERE IN LOOKED MUCH THE same as the one that had led into the echo chamber. With flashlights in hand, Gabriel and Sammi ducked their heads and walked along in single file. The passage twisted and turned and at one point became so constricted that they had to crawl through on their hands and knees. They emerged on the edge of a chasm, the lip wide enough to stand on but not much more than that. Past this ledge, the ground dropped away as if cut by a knife, and there was no indication that there was another ledge anywhere on the far side. Across didn't seem to be an option—only down.

Gabriel leaned over and shined his light toward the bottom. He estimated it was approximately thirty yards to the cavern floor. Not terrible for an experienced climber—but possibly a challenge for Sammi.

"Think you can do it?" he asked her.

"Of course. Don't be silly."

"All right. I'll go first." He removed the various tools he needed from his rucksack and laid them on the ledge. He uncoiled the rope and searched for an adequate place to anchor it. There was nothing suitable, so he took a piton with an eye and hammered it into the ledge itself. Not trusting the single piton, Gabriel grabbed two more and drove them into the rock as well. He then threaded the rope through all three eyes and tied a sturdy knot. He tugged on the rope as hard as he could to make sure the pitons would hold. Gabriel then tossed the rest of the rope over the ledge. He wasn't sure if it was long enough to reach the bottom, but it would have to do.

Gabriel showed Sammi how to put on her harness and then fastened a Petzl stop to it with a locking carabiner. He prepared his own harness the same way. Once they were in their gear and ready to go, he gave her a quick lesson on how to use the Petzl stop as a descender.

"You control your descent by applying friction to the rope that's threaded through here." He showed her how to do it. "To be safe, you want to keep it pretty tight. And take your time. We're not in a race."

"We don't know that," Sammi said. "The Corsicans could come after us at any point. Or the Egyptians."

"Only if they know the *Chant du Départ*."

"The Corsicans would," Sammi said.

"Then maybe we are in a bit of a race," Gabriel admitted. "Still. Slower but alive is better than quick and dead."

He took hold of the rope and threaded it into his Petzl stop. "I'll tell you when to start down." He then climbed over the ledge, feet first and facing the wall. He loosened the descender and slipped down several feet. Stopping, he took his flashlight and shined it all around him. There was nothing in the pit except vertical stone walls. He continued the descent and then called for Sammi to follow when he was twenty feet below the ledge. He watched as she hesitantly climbed over, dropped down and hung on the rope by her harness.

"Just hold on to the rope and use the descender."

"All right." She loosened the Petzl enough to inch down a few feet.

"Good," Gabriel said.

She opened it again, wider this time—and screamed as her harness slid down the rope at a terrifying speed. Gabriel looked up at her rapidly approaching form.

"Squeeze the Petzl!" he shouted.

She managed to do so, stopping with her feet inches from Gabriel's head.

They each took a moment to breathe.

"Sorry," she whispered.

"You all right?"

"I think so."

"Take all the time you need. I'm going to keep going and get a little distance between us." He loosened his descender and rappelled down several feet. If he'd been on his own, he could have gone the whole way down in one go—he'd had plenty of experience with vertical caving and didn't need to proceed in starts and stops. But he didn't want to leave her hanging there alone.

When he was thirty feet below her, Gabriel called for her to continue. She carefully loosened the Petzl and moved down. She got the hang of it after a few tries and was soon rappelling with confidence. Gabriel reached the end of the rope and saw the bottom ten feet below him. He unfastened the Petzl and free fell to the floor, rolling as he landed.

"I'm down," he called as he stood. He shined the light up at Sammi and saw her some fifty feet above him. "Take it easy, you're doing great."

He warned her when she got near the end of the rope and explained how to unfasten the descender and drop, legs first, to the ground. She landed beside him and sprang back up.

"You okay?" he said.

"My head still hurts," Sammi said, "but that has nothing to do with the climb."

"When we get out of this, I'm going to buy you the biggest bottle of aspirin you've ever seen."

"Such a romantic," Sammi said.

Their flashlights revealed an opening in the wall at the bottom of the pit. The passage beyond led into darkness too deep for their lights to make more than a small dent. Gabriel walked in and inched forward carefully, his free arm extended to one side and his feet testing the ground before placing each step.

Once again, the passage twisted, narrowed, widened, forked. It was remarkable just how complex the internal structure of this cave system was. Gabriel was a seasoned caver and even he was having a hard time holding a mental map of the space in his head. He couldn't help thinking some of the branches and forks must have been man-made, added solely to get would-be treasure hunters who were lucky enough to make it this far well and truly lost.

It took them more than a half hour of spelunking before they finally came to the opening of another vaulted chamber. If the first one had struck Gabriel as being the size of a large bedroom, this one seemed more like a good-sized living room.

And it was full of treasure.

"My goodness, Gabriel... what is all this?"

Their lights reflected off glittering, shiny, sparkling objects made of gold and silver, jewels of all types, caches of old swords and rifles, even framed paintings. Diamonds, emeralds, rubies... coins, gold bricks... fine art... weapons...

Gabriel reached out to touch an antique carbine rifle that must have been from Napoleon's army—and stopped.

On the ground in front of it, a clothed skeleton lay horizontally, a spear skewered through its ribcage.

"Don't touch anything," he said, pulling his hand back. Sammi pulled hers back as well; she'd been about to pick up an elaborately filigreed gold cup.

He pointed the light directly at the skeleton. Swinging it around the rest of the room, he located several more. In all, there were half a dozen skeletons, each still wearing the tattered remnants of its clothing; these remains, from periods that must have spanned a hundred years, were the only clues to the identity of the unfortunate men who had made it this far and no further. Every corpse had a spear stuck through it. Gabriel looked around the room and then pointed his flashlight up towards the ceiling. It was a latticework of small circular holes.

He rummaged in his sack and found the strap that had held the rope in a coil. He balled it up and tossed it across the room at one of the paintings. The buckle of the strap jostled the frame—and a spear shot out of the ceiling. It struck the stone floor directly in front of the painting and ricocheted away.

"Trap number two," Gabriel said. "I'm guessing all this treasure is rigged."

Gabriel continued to shine the light around the

room, walking forward cautiously, taking enormous care not to touch anything. Finally they neared the room's far wall, where another inscription had been chiseled into the stone:

*Lui seul qui montre ce qui n'est pas répertorié
peut avancer.*

Sammi moved to his side and peered at the words. "'Only he who shows what is not in the inventory may advance.'"

"What is not in the inventory? What inventory?"

"It doesn't say. Just 'what is not inventoried' or 'what is not catalogued.'"

He swung his light down, illuminating a stone shelf built into the wall beneath the inscription. Sitting on the shelf was an open, empty chest the size of a small suitcase. "We have to figure out what it means."

Sammi read the inscription aloud again, first in French and then in English. "I think it must have something to do with the Napoleonic Code."

"How so?" Gabriel asked.

"You said there were three traps, correct? Well, the Napoleonic Code was divided into three books. The first has to do with People, the second was about Property, and the third... well, the third was about Acquiring Property—sort of boring stuff for lawyers." Gabriel was reminded of the text of the Rosetta Stone, about taxes and putting statues in temples. Sometimes the greatest discoveries in history had to do with boring stuff. "The first trap," Sammi went on, "with the anthem... knowing the anthem would have been one of the tests for citizenship. It would have been covered in Book One of the Code."

Gabriel shined his light around. "And you think all this…"

"Property," Sammi said. "Book Two."

"So what does Book Two have to say about property?" Gabriel said. "Other than 'Don't take it or you'll get stabbed with a spear.'"

"THE CODE DEFINED WHAT WAS DESIGNATED AS A French citizen's personal property as opposed to what was owned by the state." Sammi looked around at all the accumulated wealth, all untouchable. "Or by the emperor."

Gabriel thought about that. "So this is *his* property. We're not allowed to take it. We have to show something that is not on his list of property to get out of here."

"But show it to whom?" Sammi said.

Gabriel bent to examine the chest and the shelf it sat on. The two seemed to be attached in some way—at least he wasn't able to move the chest off. And when he pressed down gently on the shelf, it had some give, almost like the balance of a scale.

"I think we have to put it in here—it's a receptacle. Like the hopper of a machine. You put something in, and—" He tested the chest's lid; it moved on surprisingly smooth hinges. "You put it in, close the chest, and hope you don't get a spear in your back for your troubles. The question is what goes in the chest. Just something that's our property and not his?"

"Not just anything," Sammi said. "Under the Code, 'Property' wouldn't refer to ordinary consumables or goods of minor note. It would have to be something of real value."

Gabriel looked around again. "Something like

what's on display here, only ours rather than his."

"Right. But—" Sammi took in the display of jewels and gold bars and framed paintings. "How could we possibly have anything like this? Unless you're carrying a painting on you that I don't know about?"

"Nope."

"Or a gold bar...?"

"I'm sure Michael's got some back home, in a safe deposit box somewhere. But that won't do us any good down here."

Sammi was digging through her rucksack, trying to find anything that might work. But no amount of pitons and carabiners would do.

Gabriel thought about it. His Bulova A-11 wristwatch was worth a decent amount; his Zippo lighter, too, since it dated back to World War II. But there was a second problem, beyond the question of whether they were valuable enough—whatever he put in the chest also had to be something the two-hundred-year-old mechanism, whatever it was, would somehow be able to recognize. And he didn't think Napoleon's engineer could possibly have forseen wristwatches and Zippo lighters.

"Hang on," Gabriel said. "I have an idea."

"What?" Sammi said.

"Just stay back. If I'm wrong, I don't want you getting hit, too." He positioned himself directly in front of the chest. Looking up, he saw the circular openings through which spears might shoot at any moment.

"What are you going to do?"

"I'm going to show Mr. Bonaparte some property and see what happens."

"Gabriel, please be careful–I don't want to see you hurt."

"Neither do I." Slowly he stepped forward. And

taking his Colt out of its holster, he set it down on the bottom of the chest.

It was a gun—and there were guns on display here. What's more, it was an antique; the provenance was a bit murky, but the man he'd gotten it from had sworn it had once belonged to either Wyatt Earp or Bat Masterson. Now, that would have been around 1870, not 1800... but at least it was the right century. He gave the pistol a last lingering look. If this worked it might be the last time he'd see it—and if it didn't work it might be the last time he'd see anything...

He swung the top of the chest shut and shot a glance up at the ceiling, poised to leap left or right at the first sign of motion.

But the motion, when it came, came from the wall beside the chest. With a loud grinding noise, two of the giant stone blocks slowly rotated as one until they sat perpendicular to their original position. The opening revealed a chamber on the other side.

"I don't believe it," Sammi said. "How could it possibly have known what you put in...?"

"Maybe it didn't. Maybe anything the same weight would have worked."

She looked around at the speared skeletons on the ground. "Somehow I doubt it."

"Well, then you might want to get over here, before this thing changes its mind."

He stepped forward, cautiously watching the holes in the ceiling as he passed through the opening—but no spears came.

Sammi followed carefully in his footsteps, not deviating from his path by so much as an inch. As she reached the rotated wall, the top of the chest slowly and silently rose. She looked inside. "The gun's still there," she said. She reached in to get it.

"Don't!" Gabriel shouted—but she lifted the Colt out of the chest without any ill effect.

She held the gun out to him. "What—do you think you are the only one permitted to take risks?" she said. "Besides, it wasn't all that much of a risk. Napoleon was a tyrant, but he was not a thief. He might take another man's country—but not his property."

Gabriel took the Colt and returned it to his holster. "Thank you. I can tell you, I feel a lot safer with this old friend on my hip."

"Don't get too comfortable," Sammi said. "Look."

She directed her flashlight's beam toward the ground. In the previous room there had been half a dozen human skeletons. Here, the entire floor was littered with them, many of them horribly contorted, their bony hands clutching at their skeletal throats. Here, circular holes did not just cover the ceiling, they lined the walls and floor as well. And at the far end of the chamber was a metal cage containing a stone tablet. The tablet was covered from top to bottom with minute carvings and inscriptions.

The Second Stone.

22

THE RELIC SAT ON THE ROTTED REMNANTS OF A brown cloth. It was only a fraction the size of the Rosetta Stone but its surface was covered with a similar profusion of minuscule writing, rows of angular Greek characters alternating with stretches of hieroglyphics. It was just as Amun had described, and as Louis' secretary had sketched in the document Gabriel had seen.

But just at the moment it wasn't the main thing commanding their attention.

"What do you think killed them?" Sammi said, playing her light over the skeletons scattered across the ground.

"Not spears this time," Gabriel said. "I'm guessing poison. Probably gas." He leaned forward gingerly and bent to examine one of the holes in the wall nearest to them. There was a dark, solid residue around the edges. With a bit of effort he was able to scrape some of the residue off with his fingernail. He sniffed it and grimaced.

"Sulfur dioxide," he said. "Not the strongest poison, but enough of it in a closed space will kill you."

Sammi nodded. "There were stories that Napoleon used sulfur dioxide to put down slave rebellions in Haiti and Guadeloupe. Supposedly he had gas chambers built into the holds of slave ships."

"Charming," Gabriel said. "I'm liking him more and more."

He put down his rucksack and gestured for Sammi to take hers off as well. Then he placed the bags just inside the entrance, where they'd be in the way if the wall started to rotate closed.

Carefully, they picked their way across the room, avoiding stepping on any of the skeletons.

The cage at the far end would have been large enough to hold a large dog, with bars spaced close enough to one another to prevent the Stone from being taken out, even sideways. There was a door on the front of the cage with a metal pedestal beside it, and at the top of the pedestal was a basin. There was what looked like a drain in the center of the basin—but no sign of any source of liquid. Beside the drain were some old coins.

Looking back at the cage, Gabriel saw that there was no handle on the door and no lock—at least no conventional lock.

"The basin must contain the mechanism to open the door," he said.

"Maybe you have to put something in it," Sammi said, "like with the chest outside."

"Not coins, apparently." He picked out the three tarnished specimens from the bottom of the basin.

They were Italian lire dating back seventy-five years. "At least not Italian ones."

"I don't suppose the gun would work again," she said.

"Not likely," Gabriel said. "And I don't think we'd get a second chance. I assume putting the wrong thing in triggers the gas."

He shined his light on the wall behind the cage. Once again there was an inscription:

Lui seul qui contracte un contrat français peut continuer.

"Only he who enters into a French legal contract may proceed," Sammi translated.

"Maybe you'd better tell me a bit more about Book Three," Gabriel said.

She repeated the words of the inscription to herself. "Basically it goes into detail about how property can be acquired: succession, wills, loans, mortgages, even marriage—and all of these involve contracts."

"And here we are, trying to acquire some property," he said, gesturing toward the cage. "What does it say about entering into a contract?"

She closed her eyes. "I'm trying to remember. I took a course on the Code, but that was years ago."

He bounced the coins in his palm. "Probably does involve money."

"Not necessarily," Sammi said. "There does not need to be consideration for a contract to exist under Napoleon's code—a 'meeting of the minds' or 'agreement of the wills' is sufficient. If I agree to sell something and you agree to buy it, that's a binding legal contract even if no money has changed hands."

"But if you're not here to agree," Gabriel said. "Say,

because you died two hundred years ago. If I wanted to enter into a contract with you then…?"

"Yes, there might need to be consideration exchanged in that case. As a demonstration of good faith."

"A demonstration of good faith," Gabriel said. "Or else there's no contract. So basically if we want to get the Stone out, we need to put up some money. And not lire, because a French legal contract calls for good French money." He cast a glance back toward the other room. "There's probably some back there. The problem is, we can't take it without getting skewered."

Sammi started unbuttoning her shirt.

"What are you doing?" Gabriel said.

She lifted the chain that hung between her breasts, the one she'd shown him over dinner in Nice. At first he'd thought the object on the end was a medallion—but she'd explained it was a single French franc.

A French franc from 1800.

"Of course," Gabriel said, his eyes sparking. But then he hesitated. "But are you sure? You said your mother gave it to you—"

"You have a better idea?" Sammi said. "I didn't think so." She unclipped the circular setting the coin was mounted in from the chain and with some effort popped the coin out. She laid it in his palm and closed his fingers over it.

"One franc," he said. "I wonder if it's enough."

"To buy a priceless artifact, no," she said. "But to create a binding legal contract, yes."

He nodded. It made sense—as much as any of this made sense.

He held the franc over the hole in the pedestal. Even with his flashlight aimed directly down, he could see nothing inside except blackness. "Maybe you should wait in the other room—"

"With the spears, you mean?" Sammi said. "I'm staying with you."

"All right." He dropped the coin into the hole. It clanked against the sides as it went down, and then landed on a metal surface. Machinery of some sort creaked into motion inside the pedestal, rattling the coin against what sounded like a metal pan. The sound reminded Gabriel of the mechanical coin boxes they had on New York City buses when he was a kid, the ones that sorted different types of coins from one another: halves from quarters, nickels from dimes. You'd put in a handful of change and the mechanism would decide if you'd put in the right amount. There was always someone who insisted on dropping in pennies, or Canadian money, which the mechanism wasn't built to handle, and the line would back up out the door.

But no one got gassed for it.

Gabriel felt the muscles of his back and shoulder tense. From the expression on Sammi's face, she was feeling the same. He looked over at the entryway. Maybe they both should leave while they could—

The sound stopped.

And a hissing began.

"Gabriel!" Sammi cried.

"No, wait," Gabriel said, "that's not gas, it sounds like… hydraulics."

As they watched, the pedestal swung away from the cage, and then with a click the door of the cage swung open.

Gabriel released a breath he hadn't realized he'd been holding. He approached the cage and gently reached into it. He put one hand on either side of the

Stone. Its surface was rough beneath his fingers. And the weight—it must have weighed over a hundred pounds. But he lifted it and brought it out, cradling it in his arms.

It was extraordinary. Nearly two thousand years old, and untouched by human hands since Napoleon's time. A piece of history, literally.

"Well done, my friend."

The resonant voice boomed throughout the chamber. Gabriel and Sammi spun to face it.

Reza Arif stood with several armed men behind him. Kemnebi was among them, and he had a 9mm Glock pointed at Gabriel's head. The others held rifles.

Arif came forward. "How nice to see you again, Gabriel. And you, my dear. I do so regret that we didn't meet under better circumstances." He plucked the handkerchief from his breast pocket and unfolded it, laid it across his palms. "Now, Gabriel. You give me the Stone."

23

"AS SOON AS MICHAEL TOLD ME HE'D CONTACTED you, I knew it was a mistake," Gabriel said.

Arif shrugged. "What can I say? Your family has always paid me well... but the Alliance of the Pharaohs pays better."

"You bastard," Sammi said. "You cowardly—"

Gabriel shook his head. "Sammi. Don't."

"Well, he is!"

Arif grinned at her. "You are right. I make no bones about it. I am not brave, like your friend here. If you like, you may call me a coward. But cowards live to toast the memories of brave men. As I shall toast yours, Gabriel. And yours, my dear Miss Ficatier." He shook his head. "It would have been a true pleasure to have some more time alone with you. Imagine if it had been she in my cellar instead of you all those years ago, eh, Gabriel? We would not have spent the days and nights just drinking tea."

"How did you get down here?" Gabriel said.

"Why, we followed you, of course. You left a fine trail. Even left that rope attached for us. Most helpful."

"But the first trap, the room with the echo—"

"Yes, that," Arif said. "Quite an intricate contraption, I am sure. But nothing several pounds of dynamite couldn't deal with, now that the Corsicans were no longer around to interfere."

"They're all…?"

"Dead, yes, every one of them," Arif said. "It is just us now, Gabriel. You and I and these gentlemen here. There is no one to protect the Stone now. But never fear. The Alliance will see that it returns to its rightful home."

"Don't give it to him, Gabriel!"

"If you prefer, Miss Ficatier, I'm sure Kemnebi here would be happy to take it from him."

"No," Gabriel said. There were five of them, four with guns drawn, against the two of them, Sammi armed with a flashlight and Gabriel with his hands full. "You win," he said. "Take it."

"Gabriel!"

"I just want your word that Lucy will be released unharmed, as Amun promised."

"My word?" Arif clucked and sadly shook his head. "You know what my word is worth, Gabriel."

"And you know you can name your price," Gabriel said. "Michael will pay it."

"Now, that I will have to think about most seriously." He stepped forward. "The Stone, please."

Gabriel handed it to him. Arif bent under the weight and Gabriel leaped forward, swinging his arm up and around the smaller man's throat—but Arif ducked and darted backwards out of reach. Two of the other men stepped forward to flank him.

"Now, now. That wasn't sporting." Arif passed the stone to one of the men, who carried it from the chamber.

"As for your sister, Gabriel... I am afraid Khufu has grown quite fond of her. I seriously doubt he will let her leave his side. He has wanted an heir for some time. Do you happen to know if she is fertile?"

Gabriel rushed at him. But before he could reach Arif, Kemnebi stepped between them. He blocked Gabriel's charge with one arm, lifting him off his feet and hurling him to the side. Gabriel landed on one of the skeletons in a clatter of breaking bones. He only hoped that none of them were his.

"Goodbye, Gabriel; Miss Ficatier." Arif backed out of the chamber, followed by Kemnebi and the others. "The Alliance thanks you once again for your service," he called from the other room. "Your contribution will not be forgotten."

Gabriel jumped to his feet as he saw the wall begin rotating shut. But before he could reach it, Kemnebi gave the blocks of stone a huge shove—and kicked the two rucksacks out of the way. The wall slammed closed with a sound like a kettle drum booming.

Gabriel raced to the wall and began hammering against it with his fists. He pushed at it, kicked it. Nothing. It was locked firmly in place.

"*Hey, Arif,*" he shouted, "*why don't you pick up some treasure on the way out?*"

He listened for the sound of a spear being triggered, but heard nothing. He wasn't sure he would—with the wall as thick as it was, they probably hadn't heard him shouting, either.

He returned to where Sammi stood, in the center of the room.

Was her flashlight dimmer than it had been? It was

probably just an illusion, he knew; but before much longer it wouldn't be. Darkness would come, and then thirst, and hunger, all steps along the path to becoming the two freshest skeletons on the chamber floor.

"I'm sorry, Sammi," Gabriel said. "I wish I hadn't dragged you into this."

"You didn't drag me anywhere. I made my own mind up every step of the way." She laughed ruefully. "I wish I hadn't come, but that doesn't make it your fault."

She began walking around the perimeter of the room, peering at each wall, then examining the floor, then looking up at the ceiling. She searched around the base of the cage and the track on which the pedestal had swung.

"What are you doing?" Gabriel said.

"What I do best," she said. "Finding a way out."

"We know the way out," he said. "It's the way we came in."

"We know *one* way out. Since that way is no longer available to us, I am finding another."

"Here's the other," Gabriel said, and pulled the compact pickaxe out of one of the rucksacks Kemnebi had kicked out of the way of the closing door. "It may take a while, but—"

"It'll go faster if you bring that over here," Sammi said.

She'd reached into the cage and pulled out the rotting fragments of cloth on which the Second Stone had rested. Pushing down on the bottom of the cage showed some give in the surface, like the bottom of a wrestling ring or a gymnastics mat. It wasn't solid stone.

"Well, now, that's interesting," Gabriel said.

"Isn't it?"

Gabriel leaned into the cage and started working

at the bottom surface with the point of the axe. It was slow going, but after working through a layer of stone and a layer of some sort of dense batting below, he found what seemed to be a metal panel. The edges of the panel extended a good two inches beyond the stone in which the cage's bars were embedded, but by prying with the axe and using the handle as a lever—

The center of the panel bowed and bent, and then the edge came free.

Gabriel heaved, bending the metal further back.

Beneath it, darkness beckoned.

Gabriel shined his light down, revealing a set of narrow stone rungs carved into the rock.

"How did you know…? What made you think there might be something under the cage?"

"Two reasons," Sammi said. "First, there had to be some other room connected to this one—if nothing else, a place where the mechanism for generating and propelling the poison gas was located. Perhaps also a back door through which the Corsicans could keep an eye on the Stone without having to navigate the three traps themselves."

"And the second reason?"

"My father was a magician, Gabriel. He used plenty of cages. He escaped from them. He taught me to escape from them. One thing I learned was, if you ever see a cage? There's a good chance there's something hidden under it."

24

GABRIEL WENT DOWN FIRST. THE CRUDE LADDER carved into the wall led to a chamber of roughly the same dimensions as the room above except that it was half the height. Gabriel crouched and shined his light up at the low ceiling. There was a rats' nest of narrow metal pipes, one connected to each hole in the floor above, each tube winding its way back to a central unit that looked like an enormous cast-iron pot-bellied stove. The ceiling was reinforced by wooden beams, after the fashion of a mine shaft, and the air stank of sulfur, like a room in which a thousand matches had been struck.

Next to the foot of the ladder, Gabriel's flashlight revealed a narrow tunnel leading off into the darkness. He called for Sammi to come.

The tunnel had a different smell, but no less unpleasant: it was dank and smelled of mildew and rot. And at every turn there were spider webs. Gabriel cut through them with the blade of the axe. Sammi shuddered as the torn edges of one brushed her cheek.

"So many webs," she said.

"We're underground," Gabriel said. "It's where spiders like to live."

"Don't tell me that," she said.

"They're generally harmless," Gabriel said. "If you don't bother them." He brushed away another web that stretched from top to bottom in the narrow tunnel. In the beam of their lights, a few dozen tiny spiders scattered.

"Is it normal for there to be that many?"

"They're babies," Gabriel said. "Probably freshly hatched." He swung the flashlight around from wall to wall. Another few dozen were on either wall. "Nothing to worry about." Then he swung the light up.

The underside of the tunnel's roof was a solid mass of crawling spiders, a herd of thousands—maybe tens of thousands—crawling quickly along the ceiling over their heads. They were much larger than the babies. Many were the size of quarters, some as big as half-dollars. They were moving in a way that reminded Gabriel of fire ants, crawling over one another in a desperate chaotic frenzy. And where the light struck them—

They began to drop.

Sammi screamed.

Even Gabriel emitted a startled cry and began slapping at his chest to brush them off.

But they kept coming. They were swarming the tunnel walls, ceiling, and floor.

Gabriel pushed Sammi ahead of him. "*Run*," he said through clenched teeth; and they did, batting at their clothes and hair as they went, frantically brushing the spiders away.

The tunnel forked and the branch they took began sloping upwards as they ran. The angle increased until they were almost climbing. It took a tremendous amount of strength in their legs to keep ascending at this pace—but if they'd needed an extra incentive, they had one, as some of the spiders had by now worked themselves inside their clothes and begun biting.

Sammi yelped with pain. Gabriel cursed and slapped at his skin.

They continued to climb, as fast as they were able. Gabriel lost track of how far they'd gone; it took him by surprise when they suddenly fetched up against the end of the tunnel. A dead end, sloping directly upwards. Packed earth above their heads.

Gabriel struck at the barrier with the pickaxe. Dirt and rocks crumbled down, covering them. But the material was soft and easy to break through. Sammi continued to brush the spiders off her body and his while Gabriel dug vertically, climbing on the accumulated dirt as it piled up.

A large clod of earth came down, revealing an open hole—and sunlight.

He enlarged the hole with two more swings of the axe, then lifted Sammi bodily out of the hole. He followed and ripped off his shirt, panting from exertion and pain. She'd done the same, and he saw that her chest and back were covered with painful-looking welts and bites. The bugs they'd brought up with them dropped to the ground and fled back to the darkness of the hole.

"Madam! Are you all right?"

Gabriel turned to see the source of the voice—a middle-aged British matron in sandals and sunglasses, with a compact digital camera dangling from a strap around her wrist. A man stood beside her, goggling at Sammi, who grabbed up her shirt and held it in front of her.

"Yes...yes, I'm all right," Sammi said, wincing. "Thank you."

"Henry! Don't stare!" The man stopped goggling, though he continued to sneak glances out of the corner of his eye.

Gabriel looked around. They were in the middle of the circle of menhirs—the Western Monument—at Filitosa.

"You were so right, sweetie," he said, sweeping one arm around Sammi's shoulders, "we were supposed to turn left. You two be careful—you do *not* want to get separated from your tour group."

"Oh, dear," the woman said as Gabriel led Sammi out of the circle. "Did you hear that, Henry?"

THE STAFF AT THE REPOSITORY MUSEUM DUG OUT A first aid kit and used up two tubes of hydrocortisone cream on their bites. The spiders here were not poisonous, the agent assigned to them assured Gabriel. The bites would itch and be bothersome for a few days, but...

Where, the agent wanted to know, had they come across such a large nest of spiders?

Gabriel waved his hands and made up an answer that would send them off in the wrong direction entirely. Let them fumigate some other part of the grounds. Couldn't hurt.

"Listen," Gabriel said, "can I use your phone?"

"Of course," the agent said. "Local call or long distance?"

"Long distance. New York."

The agent handed over a cordless handset and pushed two buttons on it. The dial tone started buzzing.

Gabriel dialed the Foundation.

"Gabriel!" Michael said. "Where have you been? I've been trying to—"

"Not now, Michael. I can't talk. I'll tell you more when I can." He glanced over at the museum agent. She was looking the other way, but it was clear she was still listening. "The object we discussed… it's not there anymore. It's on its way back to Amun and his crew."

"In Marrakesh?" Michael said.

"Presumably."

"I'll try to reach Arif again—"

"You might not want to do that," Gabriel said. "He's the one who took it."

Michael was silent. "Arif?"

"Yes," Gabriel said. "Arif. And if you want some even better news, he says Lucy's about to become a pharaoh's bride."

"Gabriel… you've got to do something."

"I will. I just need you to do something for me first."

"Anything."

"Have Charlie ready to fly at Ajaccio in thirty minutes. Can you do that?"

"Of course."

"And Michael?"

"Yes?"

"Tell him this one time it's okay to take any risks he wants."

25

IT WAS AFTER MIDNIGHT. THE STREETS OF MARRAKESH were dark and empty, although there were candles flickering in some windows, the illumination of a few modern street lamps, and the light of stars in the moonless sky to make their surroundings visible. As in all cities, a few homeless people were curled up in doorways and alcoves, trying to steal an hour or two of sleep. No one else was on the street at this hour.

From the outside, the building that housed the Alliance of the Pharaohs was darker than most—the windows had been boarded up again, and to a casual observer it would have looked completely deserted. But with his ear pressed to the planks nailed over the doorway, Gabriel could hear sounds of movement inside.

Well, it had been too much to hope that they'd all have been asleep. But at least they probably wouldn't be going in and out of the building too much at 1AM.

He led Sammi into the dormant square, where shuttered stands stood darkly against the blue-black sky, looming like the menhirs in Corsica. They found their way silently to the back entrance of Nizan's shop. One light was burning inside, and through a half-closed set of blinds they could see Nizan himself, seated at a desk, poring over a ledger.

Gabriel re-checked his Colt unnecessarily; it was fully loaded with six rounds and he had plenty of extras in a pouch on his belt. Sammi was armed as well, having obtained a Browning 9mm semi-automatic from Charlie. It was Foundation property, but the message from Michael seemed to have gotten across. Charlie had given her the gun and two spare magazines and showed her how to load them.

"Stick to the plan," Gabriel said. "You stay on the ground floor and watch the tunnel entrance. I'll head upstairs. Lucy's the first priority. When I've got her, I'll bring her down and you can get her the hell out of there."

"I wish you'd come with us."

"If I don't take care of the Alliance now, we'll all be watching over our shoulders for them for the rest of our lives. Which may not be very long."

"I know," Sammi said. "But I hate leaving you alone in there."

"Well, you don't have to worry about that," Gabriel said drily. "The last thing I'll be is alone."

The couple crept toward Nizan's. Keeping their backs to the wall and pistols in hand, they slipped in through the shop's rear door.

Nizan's eyes widened when he looked up and saw them. Gabriel's Colt jabbed into his neck before he could set off any alarm.

"Not a sound," Gabriel ordered.

Sammi picked up a spool of cord used to tie carpet rolls and swiftly bound Nizan's wrists and ankles, her knots expert and tight. There'd be no working his way loose from these knots; even a seasoned escape artist would have had difficulty slipping them. Gabriel fashioned a gag out of a small strip of carpet and deposited Nizan on the washroom floor, then pushed two heavy rolls of carpet in front of the door so it couldn't be opened.

With Nizan secured, they walked to the back room where the trap door was located. Gabriel threw back the carpet and dragged the door open. They went down the steps and into the tunnel, moving quickly. They reached the other building's basement in less than two minutes. Gabriel cocked his head to listen at the foot of the stairs. There were no sounds from above. He climbed the steps and slowly raised the door an inch or two. A glance told him no one was in the pantry—but now he did hear voices, from the next room over.

Gabriel mouthed the word, "Quiet," and gestured for Sammi to follow. They climbed out of the tunnel, taking care to make no sound and leaving the trap door open for a quick retreat.

Gabriel peered around a corner into the living room, then jerked back. Kemnebi was standing there, his broad back to Gabriel, lecturing two other Alliance men in Arabic. One of the other men said something back in what sounded to Gabriel like an apologetic tone. Kemnebi responded with no sympathy in his voice at all. Gabriel heard footsteps receding as the men walked out of the room.

He gestured to Sammi to remain by the door, and stepped into the living room.

Where he walked right into Kemnebi.

The other men had gone—but not him.

Kemnebi was startled, but just for a moment. He reacted with lightning speed, seizing Gabriel's gun hand before he could pull the trigger of his Colt. Gabriel punched him as hard as he could with his other hand, landing a blow to Kemnebi's solar plexus that would have felled most men. Kemnebi felt it— Gabriel could see it in his reaction—but he shook it off and kept squeezing Gabriel's hand mercilessly.

Gabriel swung a leg up between Kemnebi's legs, and that had more of an effect. The big man stumbled a few steps backward and bent over, struggling to catch his breath. Gabriel took the opportunity to deliver a second kick, this one a roundhouse to the side of his head. Kemnebi fell against a table, tipping it over and knocking all its contents to the ground.

He saw Sammi peer out from the pantry, a look of concern on her face. From upstairs came the sound of running footsteps.

"So much for stealth," Gabriel said.

Sammi whipped out the Browning and took a bead on Kemnebi's head. "Don't move."

"I'm going upstairs," Gabriel said. "Can you handle him?"

"Yes," she said, and pulled the trigger. A spray of blood stained the wall. Kemnebi slumped to the ground, dead.

"Jesus," Gabriel said. "Remind me never to make you mad."

"They're not playing around," Sammi said. "We can't either." But her hands were shaking.

Three men in three days. Gabriel tried to push the thought out of his mind. There'd be time for that sort of thinking later. Or there wouldn't, if he let himself be distracted by it now.

He sprinted to the staircase and took the steps two at a time. One of the guards met him coming down as he and Gabriel both reached the first landing. The guard delivered a haymaker to Gabriel's chin, which stunned Gabriel for a moment, but he dropped into a defensive crouch and shook off the blow. As the man came in for a second try, Gabriel blocked the punch with his forearm and gave one right back, slamming his knuckles into the man's temple. The man collapsed against the staircase banister, which snapped under his weight. He fell screaming to the floor below.

Another guard appeared on the stairs, but a pair of bullets from Gabriel's Colt sent him scurrying back upstairs. Gabriel followed, shooting one more time, and then turned off at the landing for the third floor. He raced down the hall to Lucy's room. It was shut and locked. He banged loudly on the wood with his fist. "Lucy? You in there?"

"Gabriel?" She didn't sound normal.

Gabriel lifted his boot and kicked the door in, snapping the lock off the jamb.

Lucy was there, dressed exactly as she had been in the airport, her eyes slightly glazed from the lingering effects of whatever drug they'd given her this time.

"You came back," she said, her voice muzzy.

"Of course I did," Gabriel said. "We're going to get you out of here."

"Don't think I can climb…" she said.

"You don't have to. Just stay behind me and do what I say."

"Okay… Gabriel?"

"What?" he said, and began pulling her toward the door.

"I don't hate Michael," she said sleepily. "I don't."

"That's great. We'll talk about it later."

"I just… can't live there, in their home, spending their money…"

"Later," Gabriel said. Then he pressed her back against the wall and followed suit himself just as a spray of bullets came whizzing past.

"Gabriel!" Lucy exclaimed.

He poked the nose of the Colt around the doorframe and snapped off one shot. Then another—and this time he heard someone groan and collapse. "Come on." He pulled Lucy with him toward the stairs.

They made it halfway down.

26

TWO GUARDS MET THEM ON THE SECOND FLOOR
landing. One of them held a lit oil lamp, the other a
long-barreled pistol. Both men attacked Gabriel as he
pushed Lucy out of the way. Gabriel focused on the
man with the gun. He feinted at the man's face, then
grabbed his forearm and used it as a lever to throw
the man over his shoulder. The man fired his gun as
he flew through the air and through the smashed
stair railing, plummeting to join his colleague on
the floor below. His bullet thunked solidly into the
wooden wall.

By then, the second guard was swinging the oil
lamp at Gabriel.

Gabriel ducked and slammed into the guard's
middle. The guard collapsed and the oil lamp went
flying. It crashed onto the carpeted floor, spilling its
contents and immediately igniting the area in flames.

Gabriel heard Sammi shouting from the first floor. A

few seconds later, she appeared on the staircase, trying to see through the curtain of flame that had erupted.

"Cifer!" she called.

Lucy's head jerked up. "Sammi?"

Sammi ran to her and wrapped Lucy in her arms. She helped her to her feet.

"You were supposed to stay downstairs," Gabriel said.

"You sounded like you could use some help." She looked at the smashed railing and the guard lying prone and moaning on the landing. "Guess not."

"Just get her to safety," Gabriel said. "You, too."

"You don't have to tell me twice," Sammi said, and led Lucy swiftly through the flames.

Gabriel took a moment to reload his gun, then ran down to the first floor himself. As he passed the pantry, he saw that the trap door was now closed. Good. He ran in the other direction, toward the corridor leading to Khufu's temple.

One more guard stood in the corridor. As Gabriel ran toward him, the man raised his pistol to fire, but Gabriel beat him to the draw, and the man went over backwards with a bullet in his chest.

Gabriel leaped over the guard's body and rushed to the fake stone slab that served as a door. It swung open when he grabbed the hidden handholds and pushed.

As he stepped into the temple, Khufu's back was to him. He was still in the ancient Egyptian garb, and he was placing items of value—statuettes and jewel-encrusted treasures—into a large steamer trunk. His scepter was leaning against the throne.

Gabriel aimed the Colt at the center of Khufu's back and thumbed back the hammer. Khufu stiffened and slowly straightened, extending one arm toward the side.

"Reach for that scepter and you're dead," Gabriel said.

Khufu stopped moving. With his arm halfway extended and his back still turned, he spoke. "You are a very foolish man, Mister Hunt. You should never have returned here."

"That's what everyone keeps telling me," Gabriel said.

"What do you want? Your sister? Very well. You can have her."

"I already have her," Gabriel said. "I want the Stone."

"That you cannot have," Khufu said.

"Your men are dead," Gabriel said. "Kemnebi, the guards. I don't know where Arif is, or Amun, but if they were in the building I think they'd have shown by now. You're on your own."

Khufu whirled and leaped for the scepter, snatching it up just ahead of the bullet Gabriel had sent speeding toward it. Khufu dived behind the throne.

Gabriel raced forward, keeping the throne between him and Khufu—and between him and the deadly scepter. Behind him he heard the sound of crackling flames and smelled heavy, acrid smoke. The whole place was going up in flames.

"Come on out," Gabriel called. "It's over. Give up while you can."

He expected some response—defiance, taunting, rage, an attack. But when he got no response at all, Gabriel ran around to the back of the throne. There was no sign of Khufu anywhere.

He spun in place, gun raised. Where could the man have gone?

He glanced back at the open doorway. The corridor

beyond was completely engulfed now, the cast resin walls melting from the heat. Smoke was billowing into the room at an alarming pace.

He returned to the throne. He knew the man had been here; people didn't just disappear. Khufu had to have gone *somewhere*...

He remembered what Sammi had said about cages. Maybe the same held true for thrones. He searched the elevated base of the throne carefully. Near the edge of one of the six shallow steps on which the throne rested, he spotted a very narrow tile that was raised slightly above the ones on either side. He depressed it with one finger and the steps opened on a hidden hinge.

Gabriel stuck his gun inside and pulled the trigger twice, then lowered himself to the floor and slipped into the opening.

He dropped for about ten feet, landing in a crouch on the floor of a small room lit with hanging electric lights. There was a wooden crate on casters here, its top open, its interior packed with shreds of newspaper, through the uppermost layer of which Gabriel could see one corner of the Second Stone sticking out.

And on the floor—

On the floor Khufu lay face down, blood pooling beneath him, the scepter still clutched in one hand. One of Gabriel's gunshots must have hit him, either directly or on a ricochet. Gabriel went over quickly and kicked the scepter out of his grasp.

"Hunt..." Khufu was trying to speak, but his voice was ragged and weak, muffled by the falcon mask he still wore and fading from the blood loss he'd sustained.

Gabriel squatted beside him and turned him over onto his back. The bullet had torn through his abdomen. The man was dying.

"Hunt…" he said again, and then something Gabriel couldn't make out. Gabriel reached down and pulled off the mask.

Beneath it, contorted with pain, was Amun's face.

"Mister Hunt…" Amun breathed heavily and with evident pain. "You have not won… as long as any true Egyptian breathes, men like you will… answer for their crimes…"

His voice dropped away, and his body went limp. Gabriel lifted one of Amun's arms and let it fall. This was one true Egyptian whose breathing Gabriel didn't have to worry about anymore.

Gabriel stood. Smoke was pouring into the room through the open panel in the steps of the throne, and the temperature was becoming very uncomfortable. Pretty soon it would be impossible to see, and soon after that to breathe. Gabriel looked around for an exit and spotted a door in the corner. He tried the knob and the door swung open. Gabriel went to the crate and wheeled it out.

The tunnel he found himself in looked similar to the one leading from Nizan's to the Alliance's building, and he wasn't entirely surprised when, after angling upwards steeply for about thirty yards toward the end, the tunnel let out (through a heavily barred wooden door) onto the rear loading platform of Nizan's shop.

Gabriel pushed the crate onward until he found himself on the street. A few people were standing around, some in nightclothes and robes, some of them barefoot, each turning to the others in an attempt to learn what was going on. Sirens were converging on the building a block away, where Gabriel could see the orange glow of the fire in the sky over the rooftops. He made his way down the block, steering the crate behind a row of trucks and cars that had hastily been parked on the scene, disgorging police and firemen to combat the chaos. A larger crowd had gathered here, in front of the blazing building.

Sammi and Lucy were among them, their faces frozen in strained expressions of concern.

Gabriel approached them, pushing the crate before him. "Ladies."

"Gabriel!"

"My god!"

They both rushed to him.

"We thought you were dead for sure," Lucy said. Her voice sounded a little clearer, as if the combination of adrenaline and cool night air were combating the effects of the drug in her system.

"How did you get out?" Sammi asked.

"Gabriel," Lucy exclaimed, looking at a seared patch on Gabriel's sleeve he hadn't even noticed himself, "you're hurt!"

"Oh, she's right—did you get burned?"

Gabriel held up a hand. "I'm all right. I'm *all right*. Really." He looked at his sleeve and the reddened skin showing beneath. "It's nothing a fifth of bourbon won't cure."

Sammi's eyes dropped to the crate and to the corner of gray stone peeking out from the packing material. "The Stone! You got the Stone."

Gabriel glanced at the emergency personnel, who were working hard to put out the fire. He held a finger to his lips.

"We can discuss it in the car," he said.

And together they wheeled the crate away, into the night.

27

THE PLANE WAS FUELED AND READY FOR TAKEOFF
from the same private airstrip at the Marrakesh airport
they had had previously used. They hadn't been able
to fit the crate in the trunk of the car, so Gabriel had
lifted the Stone out and left it with Sammi in the back
seat. He lugged it up the stairs of the plane now,
surprised not to see Charlie waiting for them at the
top of the steps. "Could use a hand here," he called—
but the cockpit door was already shut and with the
engines revving loudly it was clear that Charlie was
gearing up to start taxiing, so Gabriel carried the
heavy piece the length of the plane on his own, his
arms aching from the strain. His entire body ached,
in fact, and the options for good bourbon were few,
though he thought there might be a bottle stashed
somewhere on board.

The plane took off a few minutes later and they
soared into a pre-dawn sky that was just beginning

to turn all sorts of shades of pink and orange at the horizon. Sammi sat with her face pressed to the window, watching. Lucy sat beside her, head back and eyes shut. She wasn't asleep, since from time to time she would nod in response to something Sammi said to her in French, but she wasn't entirely awake either.

"Hey, Gabriel," Lucy mumbled.

"Yes?" he said.

"Did I say thank you yet?"

"You don't have to thank me. I'm your brother. It's my job."

She smiled. "Well, thank you anyway. You're a good brother."

"Get some sleep," Gabriel said.

They sat in silence as the Challenger tilted, turned, and then leveled at around 30,000 feet. Gabriel looked out the window and watched Marrakesh disappear from view. It would be a long while before he had any desire to revisit it. He sighed and then turned his attention to an English-language newspaper he had bought from a vending machine at the airport.

Strapped snugly into the seat beside him, wrapped in a blanket, was the Second Stone. He was tempted to unwrap it just a bit, begin looking over its inscriptions; but there would be time enough for that on the second leg of the flight, from France to New York. For now, the thing to do was just leave it alone. It had already been subjected to more handling in the past few hours than in the two hundred years before, and he didn't want to risk damaging it in some—

The plane lurched unexpectedly.

Sammi and Lucy both looked over at him.

"I'll go see if everything's okay," Gabriel answered. He unbuckled his seat belt, stood, and walked down the aisle to the cockpit door. Gabriel knocked and called, "Charlie? What's going on?"

There was no answer. Instead, the plane veered violently, knocking Gabriel off his feet and onto the seats next to him. Gabriel looked out the window. The scenery was swinging past the windows—they were changing course.

Gabriel got to his feet and tried the cockpit door. It was locked—which may have been standard operating procedure on commercial flights, but not on the Hunt Foundation's private jet.

He rapped again. "Charlie! Open the door!"

Nothing.

This isn't good.

Unlike commercial airplanes, the door to the Challenger's cockpit wasn't break-proof, so it wasn't difficult for Gabriel to raise his foot and kick the door in.

He followed the swinging door into the cockpit, then stopped dead.

Reza Arif stood inside the broken door. He held a Parabellum-Pistole in his right hand. The barrel was pointed at Gabriel's chest.

"Back up, Gabriel. Hands in the air."

"Goddamn it," Gabriel muttered. He looked past Arif and saw that Charlie had a gag tied around his mouth and his hands cinched together with a pair of plastic crowd-restraint cuffs. Somehow he was still flying the plane. "How did you get on board?"

"How did I get on board?" Arif laughed. "Do you forget the connections I have in my country? I may be wanted by the police, but that doesn't mean I can't pull strings, especially at an airport owned by my good friends in the *Union Corse.* Access to a privately owned jet at the airstrip? That's nothing." He jerked his head toward Charlie. "Your pilot has been very accommodating. He knows that if he tries anything stupid we will all die. I've instructed him to take us where I want to go."

"Where's that?"

"I don't think I'll tell you, Gabriel. You'll find out when we land. If you're still alive when we land—it's up to you."

"And then?"

"And then we shall see. First of all, I will relieve you of Second Stone, for the second time. Even though the Alliance isn't around to take it off my hands anymore, I am sure I can find a buyer willing to pay a handsome price for it. I've already had an offer of forty-five million—but I think I can get at least a hundred. Do you think the Hunt Foundation would be interested in making a bid?"

"I think the Hunt Foundation would be interested in seeing you in a jail cell. Or a morgue."

"Tsk, tsk," Arif said. "I suggest you take your seat, now, Gabriel. Oh, and please hand me your weapon. You do you still carry that revolver, don't you?"

"Better than that German piece of junk you're holding."

"What are you talking about? A Luger in fine shape is one of the most sought-after collectibles in the world. It's an excellent semi-automatic. Each magazine holds eight rounds, which is two more than your Colt. A thirty-three percent advantage." He held out his hand. Gabriel reluctantly pulled his Colt out of its holster and handed it to Arif. Arid dropped it into a carry-on bag that sat on the co-pilot seat. "Thank you. Now back your seat. And buckle up."

Gabriel scowled at him, but turned when prodded

with Arif's gun. Arif followed him back.

"My two favorite women," he said, nodding toward where Sammi and Lucy were sitting. "How nice to see you again."

"You know that shooting a pistol in here wouldn't be a very good idea," Gabriel said. "Which makes your threat a little meaningless."

"I don't see you acting like it's meaningless," Arif said. "And that's because you know the nonsense you see in the movies isn't true—that business about plummeting cabin pressure and people being sucked out through the windows. It's good for one of your James Bond pictures, but it doesn't work that way in real life.

"You're right, of course, that I don't *want* to fire the gun in here. But I will if I have to. So please, none of you do anything stupid, all right? This will all be over in a few hours. We'll land, I'll take the Stone, and you lot can go off to wherever you like, unmolested."

Gabriel's eyes narrowed. "You give your word."

Arif shrugged.

"I know you, Reza. You have no intention of letting us go. The Hunt Foundation's jet is going to mysteriously disappear, isn't that right? And its pilot and three passengers along with it."

Arif waved the Luger. "That's enough. If you want to live, I suggest you be quiet."

A new voice spoke then, coming from unseen speakers around the plane's cabin. Looking over, Gabriel saw Sammi's finger resting on one of the buttons on her armrest. The one with a picture of a telephone on it.

"*Reza,*" Michael Hunt said, "*if you touch any of them, I will personally see that you pay for it.*"

"You?" Arif said, with a laugh. He looked up at the plane's ceiling, as though that's where the voice was coming from. "Michael Hunt, with your books and your scrolls and your ancient languages? What will you do, Michael, bore me to death?"

"Don't underestimate me, Reza," Michael said. "You're not the only shady operator I know."

"'Shady operator.' You wound me, Michael, you really do. I aspired at least to 'nefarious.'" He swung the gun to point at Sammi. "Enough. Hang up on him."

Gabriel didn't need any more opportunity than that. He launched himself out of his seat and jumped at Arif, tackling him from the side. Together they tumbled into the cabin's aisle, Arif clawing at Gabriel's face, Gabriel slugging him in the neck with one hand and grabbing hold of Arif's gun hand with the other.

"What's going on?" Michael asked. "Sammi? Lucy? Somebody—"

Arif swung his free hand, connecting painfully with Gabriel's ear. Gabriel's grip on the gun loosened and Arif yanked it free. He scooted backwards and got an arm around Gabriel's throat. Gabriel grabbed hold of Arif's arm, trying to pull it off him, but a moment later felt the barrel of the Luger pressing against his head.

"I said, *enough.*" Arif was breathing heavily. "You people don't listen, do you?"

"Will somebody tell me what's happening?"

"I'll tell you what's happening, Michael," Arif said, and jabbed the gun violently against Gabriel's skull. "I am pointing a gun at your brother's head and in a moment I am going to blow his brains out. After which I'll decide just what to do with your sister. How do you like that?"

"Don't—"

Lucy unbuckled her seatbelt and stood, swaying a bit as she did.

Arif and Gabriel both spoke at the same instant. "Sit down!"

She shook her head.

And from behind her back pulled Charlie's Browning.

Sammi looked down, surprised to see the gun gone from where she'd stowed it before boarding, in the shoulder bag under her seat.

"Ah," Arif said, "so the little sister is armed. I wouldn't trust her to shoot straight, though, not drugged the way she is—would you, Gabriel?"

Gabriel looked at his sister, looked at the tip of the gun, wavering slightly in her unsteady hands. His head and Arif's were side by side. A miss by an inch would kill the wrong man.

"She's a Hunt, you son of a bitch," Gabriel said. "I'd trust her with my life." And he nodded slightly.

Lucy pulled the trigger.

28

ARIF'S GRIP SLACKENED.

Gabriel released himself from it, throwing the dead man's arm to one side. Arif slumped in the aisle as Gabriel stood.

Lucy's hands had dropped, the gun sliding from them to the floor. Her whole body was shaking. Gabriel took her in his arms. As he did, she started to cry.

"Damn it," Michael said, "somebody tell me what's going on!"

"It's okay," Sammi said. "Everything's okay."

GABRIEL FINISHED CARRYING OUT THE LAST BAGS OF garbage from Lucy's apartment and sat down on the couch. They had been in Nice for twenty-four hours, doing nothing but restoring her home to its original condition. Practically everything had to be junked. She needed a new computer, new furniture, a new paint job. There was a lot of work still to be done.

"Maybe I should just leave," she said, dropping down on the couch beside him. "I never stay in one place too long, and this one… let's just say the memories here aren't the best."

"I'll try not to take that personally," Sammi called from the other room.

Gabriel shrugged. "I can't tell you whether to stay, Lucy. You've always done what you wanted to do. Is there anything keeping you here?"

She rubbed her chin. "I don't know. Not really. My work I can do anywhere. There's Sammi… but you'd come with me if I decided to move to Spain, right? Or Denmark?"

"MAYBE SPAIN," SAMMI SAID, APPEARING IN THE doorway. She was wiping her hands on a rag. "Denmark's too cold."

"Or maybe you'd like to go back to New York with Gabriel," Lucy said. "I've seen the way you two have been looking at each other."

Gabriel and Sammi did look at each other then. Gabriel couldn't have said what the look in Sammi's eyes meant, or what the one in his own eyes did. He didn't plan to settle down in New York any time soon, with Sammi or anyone else—but spending some more time with her wasn't at all an unappealing notion.

A ringing coming from Gabriel's pocket broke the moment. He reached into it for the new cell phone Michael had overnighted to him. It had at least twice as many buttons on it as the last one, and no doubt had reception even if you were in outer space.

"Hello," Gabriel said, flipping it open.

"Ah, Gabriel," Michael said. "Glad to see you got the phone."

"That's sort of a funny thing to call me to check. I mean, if I hadn't gotten it and you tried calling—"

"I didn't call you to check," Michael said. "I called you to say I'm on my way."

"To Nice?" Gabriel said.

"To the third floor," Michael said. A moment later footsteps sounded on the other side of the front door. A fist knocked briskly.

Gabriel turned to Lucy.

"You set this up," she accused.

"Not me," Gabriel said. "I didn't—"

Another knock.

Gabriel closed the cell phone. "I bet he has a way of tracking this thing."

"You think?" Lucy said.

"Do you want me to tell him to go away?" Gabriel said. "I will if you want me to."

She stood. "No."

She walked to the door, swung it open.

Michael was standing there in a suit and topcoat, hands in his coat pockets.

"Hey, Michael," she said.

"Hello."

She walked back to the couch. "You can come in, but I'm warning you, the place is a mess."

Michael stepped inside. "That's okay," he said.

"I'm sorry I didn't call," she said. "For nine years."

Gabriel went over to Sammi. "Come on," he said.

"Let's go back to the place with that awful red wine, and you can finally tell me how you managed to escape from this apartment the day we met."

"A good magician—" Sammi began, but Gabriel

stopped her with a kiss. It went on for some time. When they finally separated they saw Lucy and Michael both staring at them.

"Maybe *we* should go," Lucy said, "and leave you two here."

"That's okay," Sammi said. "My apartment isn't far." She took Gabriel by the hand. "I think maybe you can get me to reveal a secret or two. If you ask very nicely."

Looking back at Michael and Lucy, seated side by side watching him, Gabriel was struck by a sudden memory of the last time he'd seen them sharing a couch. Michael had been twenty-three, Lucy seventeen. It had been nearly a decade since then, and so much had changed. And yet some things never would.

"You guys talk," he said, putting an arm around Sammi's waist. "You've got a lot of catching up to do."

ABOUT THE AUTHOR

Raymond Benson is the author of more than thirty books and was the official author of the licensed James Bond novels from 1997 to 2003, including *Zero Minus Ten* and *High Time to Kill*. His *James Bond Bedside Companion* was nominated for an Edgar Award. Other works include the Shamus Award-nominated *Dark Side of the Morgue* and he has written ten computer games, including *Stephen King's The Mist*.

ACKNOWLEDGMENTS

THE AUTHOR WISHES TO THANK GABRIEL AND Michael Hunt for allowing me to pen this exploit, as well as Peter Miller, Kevin Collette, Cornell Stamoran, Marc Wolff, everyone at Hard Case Crime, and, of course, Randi and Max.

Read on for an extract from the first

GABRIEL HUNT ADVENTURE

HUNT AT THE WELL OF ETERNITY

1

GABRIEL HUNT TUGGED AT THE TIGHT COLLAR AROUND HIS
neck and grimaced as he failed to loosen it. He stuck
the thumb of his other hand inside the cummerbund
cinched around his waist and pulled it out a little.

"I *hate* tuxedos," he muttered.

His brother Michael leaned closer to him. Without
altering the beaming smile on his face, Michael said
from the corner of his mouth, "Stop fidgeting."

"Easy for you to say, yours probably fits."

"You could have had one made as well," Michael
said. "Thomas would have been delighted. If instead
you choose to *rent* from some off-the-rack dealer..."

"Best part of wearing a tuxedo's getting to give
the damn thing back," Gabriel said. Then he spotted
something that interested him more than the collar's
constraints.

Some*one*, actually.

The loveliest woman he had seen in quite some time.

She moved toward the Hunt brothers, her natural grace allowing her to glide with apparent ease through the crowd that thronged the Great Hall of the Metropolitan Museum of Art. She was as beautiful as any of the masterpieces hung on the walls in the museum's many galleries.

A mass of midnight-black curls framed a compelling, high-cheekboned face dominated by dark, intense eyes. Those curls tumbled over honey-skinned shoulders left bare by the strapless evening gown of dark green silk that clung to the generous curves of her body. She possessed a timeless, natural beauty that was more attractive to Gabriel than anything the multitude of stick-thin, facelifted society women attending this reception could ever muster.

And she appeared to be coming straight toward him.

"Who's that?" Gabriel asked his brother.

"I have no idea," Michael replied. "I don't think I've ever seen her before."

"You'd remember if you had," Gabriel said. "I thought you knew everyone here."

Tonight's reception was in honor of a new exhibit of Egyptian art and artifacts, many of which the Hunt Foundation had provided on loan to the museum. Gabriel had brought several of those artifacts back with him from a recent trip to Egypt—some of them even with the knowledge of the Egyptian government. The exhibit would open to the public the next day, but tonight was an advance showing for the museum's wealthiest benefactors.

Gabriel snagged a couple of glasses of champagne from a tray carried by a passing waiter. The beautiful young woman might be thirsty, and if she was, he was going to be ready.

"What's that she's carrying?" Michael asked in an undertone.

It was Gabriel's turn to say, "I have no idea." Instead of some glittery, fashionable purse, the young woman carried a cloth-wrapped bundle of some sort. The cloth was a faded red, and to Gabriel's eye, it appeared old. The fabric looked distressed, the edges frayed.

A waiter moved in front of her, offering her a drink. She shook her head and looked irritated that the man had interrupted her progress across the hall. When Gabriel saw that, he tossed back the champagne in one of the glasses he held, then pressed the other into Michael's hand.

Either the lady didn't drink, or she had something else on her mind at the moment.

Gabriel set the empty glass on a pedestal supporting a clay vase, then turned to greet the young woman with a smile as she finally reached the spot where he and Michael were standing, near one of the pillars that ran along the sides of the hall.

"Señor Hunt?" she said. He caught a hint of a South American accent, but only a hint.

"That's right," Gabriel said, but before he could ask her who she was, she spoke again.

"Señor Michael Hunt?"

Gabriel shot a sidelong glance Michael's way and Michael stepped forward, smiling. Shorter, younger, and studious-looking rather than ruggedly handsome, he was accustomed to paling into insignificance next to his more dynamic older brother. But that didn't mean he had to like it.

"I'm Michael Hunt," he said. "And you are…?"

"My name is Mariella Montez," she told him.

"And what can I do for you, Miss Montez?"

Before she could reply, the waiter who had stopped her on her way across the hall appeared behind her sleek, bare left shoulder. "Excuse me, ma'am, but I believe you dropped this."

With an annoyed look again on her face, she turned toward the red-jacketed man and said, "I didn't drop anything—"

But what the waiter was extending toward her was a pistol, aimed directly between her ample breasts. He reached out with his other hand to snatch the bundle she was carrying.

Mariella jerked back and said, "No!"

Incredulous and instantly tensed for trouble, Gabriel stepped between Mariella and the waiter. "Hey, buddy, put that thing down. This is a museum, not a firing range."

"This is not your concern," the waiter said, and swung the pistol at Gabriel's head.

Instinct brought Gabriel's left arm up to block the blow. His right fist shot up and out in a short, sharp punch that rocked the waiter's head back and bloodied his nose.

With his now crimson-smeared face contorted with anger, the waiter swung again. This time he slashed at Gabriel's throat. Gabriel leaped backwards and collided with the young woman.

Such a collision might have been pleasurable under other circumstances, but not now. Not with a madman of a waiter swinging a gun that he could just as easily start firing at any moment.

Gabriel felt Mariella push him away, then say, "Señor Hunt, you must take this!" But she wasn't talking to him. He heard Michael, behind him, saying, "What is it?" She was probably trying to give Michael the cloth-wrapped bundle, whatever it was. Gabriel didn't have the time to check whether the hand-off had been successful. Instead, he lowered his head and tackled the waiter around the waist, driving the man off his feet. The gun went off as they fell, the bullet shattering a pane of glass in the ceiling twenty feet overhead.

Commotion filled the Great Hall as shards of glass rained down. Some men yelled and pushed forward, demanding to know what was going on. Others scurried out of the way, trampling on the trailing edges of their dates' expensive gowns in their rush to steer clear of the fray. Security guards ran toward the scene of the struggle.

Gabriel knocked the gun out of the waiter's hand, but the waiter darted in under Gabriel's guard, wrapped his fists around Gabriel's throat, and squeezed with a grip like a dockworker's. Gabriel heaved himself off the marble-tiled floor and rolled over in an attempt to break the man's hold. The waiter hung on stubbornly.

Rolling over and then over again, the two men crashed into a pedestal—the same pedestal, in fact, where Gabriel had placed his empty champagne glass a few minutes earlier. It fell to the ground and shattered, spraying shrapnel.

The Egyptian vase that stood on the pedestal was heavier and didn't fall immediately—but Gabriel noted with a surge of concern as it started to topple.

It wasn't fabulously rare or valuable—otherwise it would have been safely behind glass or at least velvet ropes. But it *was* old, and Gabriel watched its growing tilt with alarm.

As the vase tipped over, he let go of the waiter's forearms and shot out a hand to catch it. It landed in his palm, just an inch above the stone floor. One more inch and it would have been a pile of worthless shards, like the shattered window overhead. He lowered it gently.

Meanwhile, though, the waiter had gone on with his attempt to squeeze what little air still remained in Gabriel's lungs out of his body. A red haze was starting to form over Gabriel's vision and rockets were exploding behind his eyes from lack of oxygen. There were people all around them, but no one was reaching in to help—they seemed to be distracted by something else that was going on. Gabriel tried to call out to them, but found himself unable to get a sound out through his constricted throat.

If he hadn't been wearing a goddamn tuxedo, he'd have had his Colt on him and maybe could have gotten to it. Or at least a knife—he'd have had *something*. As it is, he had nothing, except a cummerbund, a bowtie, and maybe a half-minute of consciousness left.

Ah, hell, Gabriel thought. *Dust to dust*.

With a heave, he smashed the vase over the head of the man trying to kill him.

The waiter slumped sideways, and his fingers slipped off Gabriel's throat at last. Compared to their grip, the hated tuxedo collar suddenly felt luxurious. Gasping lungfuls of air, Gabriel sat up. He yanked his bowtie off and ripped his collar stud out, panting.

Then he took stock of the chaos all around him.

The waiter who'd attacked him wasn't the only member of the service staff that seemed to have been overtaken by violent impulses. Several more red-jacketed men had pulled guns from under their jackets and now menaced the crowd, alternating between simply brandishing the weapons and firing them over everyone's head. Smoke from their gunfire hung in the air, stinking of gunpowder and flame. Women screamed, men shouted curses, and vice versa. Everybody was scrambling to get out of the line of fire, though no two people seemed to agree on which direction was safest. As Gabriel leaped to his feet, he saw one man dive into an open stone sarcophagus. Then one of the waiters spotted a security guard leveling a gun at him and without hesitating shot the guard in the chest. Blood sprayed and the crowd screamed.

The gunman swung his automatic toward another guard. Racing up behind him, Gabriel ripped the cummerbund from around his own waist and, holding both ends, dropped it over the gunman's head from behind. He jerked back hard just as the man squeezed the trigger. The shot slammed upward toward the vaulted ceiling and another window high above them splintered.

With the cummerbund forming a makeshift lasso around the gunman's neck, Gabriel swung him face-first into one of the pillars. The crunching impact made the man go limp. Gabriel let go of one end of the cummerbund and allowed the unconscious man to fall to the floor.

Gabriel spun around to look for Michael. He caught a glimpse of his brother and Mariella at the far end of the room, fear-stricken guests dashing back and forth between him and them. Michael had the cloth-wrapped bundle tucked under one arm now, and with his other hand he held the woman's wrist, trying to guide her through the chaos.

More gunshots blasted out, increasing the panic in the room. Gabriel didn't know how many civilians had been hit so far, or whether any had been trampled in the stampede. But it was too optimistic to hope either number was zero.

From the street outside, he heard the sounds of police sirens approaching—but they sounded far away.

He started shouldering his way through the crowd in the direction of Michael and Mariella. He was still several yards away when one of the waiters appeared next to Michael and chopped at his head with a tightly held automatic. The blow landed with a hollow impact that Gabriel could hear even over the din in the vast room. Michael's knees unhinged and he fell, letting go of the woman and dropping the bundle.

"Michael!" Gabriel roared. He fought his way forward.

Mariella screamed as another waiter grabbed her and started dragging her away. She twisted in his grip and punched him, a nice solid right hook. The blow was enough to knock her assailant back a step. She lunged toward the bundle Michael had dropped.

Before she could reach it, a fleeing woman passing by kicked the bundle and sent it rolling across the floor. The cloth unwrapped as it rolled. Gabriel caught a glimpse of the object the cloth had been protecting.

A whiskey bottle.

Mariella threw herself after the bottle, grabbing for it. The waiter who had pistol-whipped Michael was after the bottle, too. He threw people aside to get them out of his way. The automatic rose and fell as he used it to batter a path through the crowd. Mariella was about to snatch the bottle from the floor as the man reached her, grabbed the back of her dress, and hauled her up and shoved her away.

Gabriel finally made it to Michael's side, bent to take hold of his brother's arm and lift him to his feet. Michael was groggy but conscious, a trickle of blood worming down his face from a deep cut in his scalp.

"Can you stand?" Gabriel had to shout to get his attention.

Michael nodded, wincing at the pain the motion must have set off inside his head. Gabriel helped him lean against a pillar and told him to stay there, then headed for Mariella.

The crowd was beginning to thin a little, and Gabriel realized that one purpose of all the shooting had been to herd the throng of guests toward the museum's front entrance, leaving more room for the waiters to go after Mariella. Several bodies lay crumpled on the floor and a few guests crouched cowering in the corners, but much of the high society crowd had already escaped and most of the remaining guests and museum staff were pressing and fighting to get out the doors.

Mariella was just fighting, period. Two more waiters had grabbed her, but they had their hands full holding her while the first one went after the whiskey bottle. She stamped on their feet and kicked at their legs and writhed in their grasp. Before Gabriel could get to her, she tore loose from her captors for a second and tackled the other waiter from behind. As he fell, his hand just missed the bottle he'd been reaching for.

"Get her off me!" the waiter roared to his associates.

The other two men latched on to her again, but by this time Gabriel was there, clubbing his hands together and smashing them into the back of one man's neck. The man went down hard, as if every muscle in his body had gone limp.

Mariella twisted and clawed at the other man's face, leaving red streaks on his cheeks. He threw his hands up as she feinted at his eyes, then she lifted a knee into his groin. He doubled over in agony.

That left only the waiter who was trying to retrieve

the bottle, and unfortunately it left him free. He grabbed for it once more.

Mariella cried, "Stop him!" as Gabriel ran past her.

The waiter scooped up the bottle and turned with a satisfied smirk on his face. The expression didn't last long because in the next second Gabriel's fist crashed into his face.

As the man teetered, Gabriel got his first good look at him. He was big, well over six feet tall, with massive shoulders that strained the seams of the uniform jacket. He hadn't gotten those shoulders carrying trays of champagne, nor was waitering likely to be how he'd acquired his broken nose or the network of scars along both cheeks and around his eyes.

The punch had momentum and all of Gabriel's weight and strength behind it. Despite being bigger and heavier than Gabriel, the man reeled from the impact. His hands went up in the air…

And the whiskey bottle flew out of his grip, turning over and over as it soared high and then came crashing down to shatter on the marble floor in an explosion of glass and liquid.

Mariella Montez had just seen several men beaten and several more shot, and she'd watched it all without showing any abnormal distress, any grief. But now, as she saw the glass shatter and its contents lost, she screamed, a low, plaintive wail, as if her heart had been ripped out.

2

IT WAS SUCH A SOUL-RENDING CRY THAT GABRIEL had to turn and look at her. She had clapped her hands to her face and her eyes were wide with horror. Before he could ask her for an explanation, Gabriel heard the scuff of shoe leather behind him.

The punch Gabriel landed as he spun would have knocked most men out cold, but not this red-jacketed plug-ugly. The man was still upright, swinging a long, brawny arm in a backhanded swipe that smashed into Gabriel's jaw. Gabriel staggered but managed to stay on his feet.

He yelled, "Michael, no!" as his younger brother came running up and jumped onto the big man's back.

The phony waiter grunted and turned in place with Michael clinging to him, then brushed Michael off like a horse swatting away a fly. As Michael fell backward with his arms windmilling, he crashed into Gabriel. Their legs tangled and both of them went down.

That gave the waiter enough time to grab Mariella, throw her over his shoulder, and start galloping toward one of the rear exits. The other waiters covered his retreat with blazing automatics. Gabriel scrambled up but couldn't give chase. Flying lead forced him to grab Michael and duck behind one of the thick pillars as slugs pitted it.

He risked a glance around the pillar when he heard Mariella scream. She was pounding her fists against her captor's back as he ran, but he didn't seem to feel the blows.

Gabriel grimaced and wished again that he'd brought a gun with him tonight. He would have risked a shot at the son of a bitch's legs to bring him down.

As it was, all he could do was pull his head back while bullets chipped splinters of plaster from the pillar next to his ear. His last sight of Mariella came as she was carried, still struggling, through the rear exit.

"The back!" a cop yelled from the front of the Great Hall. "Somebody cover the back!" Other cops were pouring into the room finally, and Gabriel saw two of them salute, turn on their heels and run out again, no doubt headed for the back.

But they would get there too late, Gabriel knew. Despite all the chaos, the waiters had sliced through the scene with brisk efficiency, like sharks through a school of minnows. Whoever and whatever else they were, they were professionals. Chances were their getaway was already arranged and they would be gone before any of the police could reach the back of the huge museum building.

Gabriel turned to Michael and said, "What the hell were you thinking, jumping on that guy?"

"I had to do something."

"You do plenty," Gabriel said. "Leave the jumping on people to me."

"What was that he was after, anyway? It was rolling and spinning around so much I never got a good look at it."

"I did," Gabriel said. "It was a whiskey bottle."

"A bottle of whiskey!"

Gabriel shook his head. "That's not what I said. Come on."

The shooting had stopped. Police officers and fire department paramedics were spreading out through the hall to check on the people who were injured.

Gabriel frowned as he scanned the room. He didn't see any of the red-jacketed figures they'd taken down during the fray. The phony waiters had taken their wounded with them.

Michael still wasn't too steady on his feet, so Gabriel kept one hand under his brother's arm as he led him toward the spot where the bottle had shattered. He knelt, touched a couple of fingers to the wet spot on the floor, and then smelled them.

"That's not whiskey," he said. Not that he'd thought it had been—whatever had been in the bottle hadn't been dark enough to be whiskey. "Doesn't smell like any other kind of booze, either."

He wet his fingers with the residue again and licked them, causing Michael to exclaim, "For God's sake, Gabriel, don't do that!"

Gabriel looked up. "Why not?"

"It could be some sort of toxin!"

Gabriel waited a moment, then shook his head. "Not a fast-acting one anyway." He tasted it again. "It has no flavor at all." He bent forward, sniffed at the spot directly. "No smell. No color. It's not oily, not viscous. As far as I can tell, it's water. Plain water."

"Some poisons are flavorless and odorless."

Gabriel nodded. "And not oily, sure. But so's water, and I think that's what this was a bottle of."

Michael raised a hand to the cut on his head, winced as he touched it. "Why all that fuss over a whiskey bottle filled with...?"

"Water?"

"They went to a lot of trouble to get it away from Miss Montez."

"Damned if I know."

"You guys freeze!"

The brothers looked up at a beefy NYPD cop with a thick mustache dangling down over his upper lip. He had a service revolver leveled at them.

"Perfect timing, officer," Gabriel said. "If you've got a key to the barn door, feel free to lock it."

"Huh?"

"The horse." Gabriel made a shooing gesture with one hand. "Gone."

The cop turned to Michael. "What's he talkin' about?"

Michael gave Gabriel a look, then said, "Officer, we're not armed, and we didn't have anything to do with what happened here. We were guests at the reception. In fact, our Foundation was co-host of the reception."

The cop nodded toward the pieces of broken glass scattered across the floor. "What's that you were monkeyin' with?"

"That bottle appears to be what the gunmen were trying to obtain," Michael said. "Along with a woman named Mariella Montez, who has been abducted."

"Who's this Montez?"

Gabriel said, "A young woman. About so tall—" Gabriel gestured with one hand. "Black hair. Busty.

One of those phony waiters carried her off just before you got here."

The cop sighed wearily. "Oh, Lord. That's kidnappin'. Means we'll have the damn FBI to deal with, too. Hey, stop that!"

Gabriel had taken a pen from his pocket and was using it to turn one of the larger pieces of broken glass over. "Look," he said to Michael. "Most of the label is still intact."

Michael leaned over and put his hands on his knees, squinting to study the label. The cop bent over beside him. "Old Pinebark," Michael read. "Brewed in… Dobie's Mill, Florida." He looked at Gabriel and shook his head. "I've never heard of it."

"That doesn't exactly surprise me, Michael," Gabriel said as he straightened. "But I haven't either. And here I thought I'd sampled just about every brand of rotgut, hooch, and Who-hit-John under the sun."

"That's hardly something to boast about," Michael muttered.

"How about you, officer? You ever hear of Old—" But looking up, Gabriel saw the policeman wasn't listening. He was staring at the cloth that had been wrapped around the bottle. It was lying on the floor of the Great Hall, wadded up and soiled from being trampled underfoot.

Gabriel walked over to it, squatted down on his haunches. There was some sort of design on the cloth. He used the tip of his pen to straighten it out.

"There you go, messing with evidence again," the cop complained.

The cloth was perhaps thirty inches square. The faded colors and some tattering around the edges indicated that it was quite old; there were long-dried bloodstains spattered along one edge and even a dark-rimmed bullet hole in one spot. Crossed sabers were emblazoned in each corner. Set in a large, gilt-edged circle that took up most of the center of the flag was a picture of a gray-uniformed man on a magnificent, rearing stallion. In the background was a large white house with white columns, set among rolling green hills and fields covered with lush crops. Letters that arched above the circle read *Fifth GA. CAVALRY*, and below the picture, set slightly apart, were the letters *C S A*.

Gabriel said, "You're the one with the history degree. Want to tell me what we're looking at?"

"It appears," Michael said, "to be the battle flag of a Confederate cavalry regiment."

"THE FIFTH GEORGIA CAVALRY WAS COMMANDED BY Brigadier General Granville Fordham Fargo," Michael said several hours later as he pointed at a yellowed page in the oversized volume spread open on the room's cherrywood reading table, itself an antique. He and Gabriel were in the Sutton Place brownstone that served as the headquarters of the Hunt Foundation, as well as Michael's home.

The brothers had spent a portion of the intervening hours being questioned by the police at the scene, but they hadn't been able to tell the cops anything beyond what was obvious: Someone had substituted gunmen for the real waiters who were supposed to serve at the reception, apparently for the purpose of kidnapping Mariella Montez and stealing the bottle she had brought with her to the museum. When the bottle shattered, they satisfied themselves with just grabbing her.

The grisly discovery of the bodies of the real

waiters in the catering van parked behind the museum provided grim confirmation. Each of them had been killed by a single shot to the back of the head. Professional executions.

Instead of returning to his own rooms on the top floor of the Discoverers League building, Gabriel had come here to the brownstone with Michael. Michael had been sorting through one musty volume after another in the library adjoining his office for over an hour while Gabriel paced impatiently. The books Michael had pulled from the shelves were stacked in neat piles on the floor and the table. Only two were open.

Gabriel reversed a chair and straddled it as Michael went on, "The Fifth Georgia was raised from a county in the southern part of the state, near the border with Florida. Just across the border is where this place Dobie's Mill was located. That also happens to be the location of the only major battle the regiment took part in, the Battle of Olustee. That was in 1864. There's a list here of all the officers who served."

"I don't guess any of them were named Montez?"

Michael shook his head. "No."

"What about that Old Pinebark distillery? You find anything about that?"

Michael hesitated. He loosened his bowtie and pulled it from around his neck, then opened his collar, which he hadn't done until now. Gabriel had long since thrown his tuxedo jacket over the back of a chair, with the tie and cummerbund stuffed in the pockets.

"That's actually rather odd," Michael said. He moved over to the second open book, turned it around so it was facing Gabriel. "According to Hogan's *History of Distilling in America*, the Old Pinebark distillery was destroyed during the war and never rebuilt."

"I don't suppose you mean World War II," Gabriel said.

"No," Michael said. "The Civil War."

Gabriel frowned. "That would mean that bottle was at least—"

"A hundred forty-four years old," Michael said with a nod.

"So we've got an antique whiskey bottle wrapped in a battle flag from the Civil War," Gabriel said.

"Yes, and if the police find out that we have them, we're going to be in trouble," Michael warned.

The cop who had questioned them at the museum had been called away by one of his superiors, and Gabriel had taken the opportunity to carry the flag over behind one of the pillars, where he quickly folded it up and stashed it at the small of his back, under his shirt. The piece of broken glass with the label attached had gone into his pocket.

The flag was now spread out on the table next to the books. The piece of the bottle rested atop the elaborately decorated cloth.

"What did you find out about Mariella Montez?"

"Nothing," Michael said. He waved in the direction of the computer sitting in one corner of the room, as out of place among the ceiling-high shelves of old books as a cell phone in a monastery. "Not even online. It's as if... she doesn't exist."

"She exists, all right," Gabriel said, thinking about the way Mariella had felt to him when he bumped into her. Though he'd been too distracted to appreciate it at the time, he wouldn't soon forget that steel-under-velvet body.

Gabriel went on, "Why'd she want to give the flag and the bottle to you?"

Michael spread his hands. "Lots of people bring antiques to the Hunt Foundation—to evaluate, to identify. To buy. Usually items of older vintage than the Civil War, true, but..."

"You think she wanted you to buy them from her?" Gabriel asked. "An old whiskey bottle full of water?"

"It may have had some sort of value other than the purely economic," Michael said, and Gabriel remembered how she'd screamed when the bottle broke.

"There's one way to find out," Gabriel said.

"How?"

"You said the distillery was in Northern Florida, near where this regiment fought its only battle...?"

"That's right," Michael said. "Olustee."

"Then it looks like I'm going to Florida," Gabriel said.

DON'T MISS ANY OF THE EXCITING ADVENTURES OF GABRIEL HUNT!

THE GABRIEL HUNT ADVENTURES

"A pulp adventure series with classic style and
modern sensibilities… Escapism at its best."
Publishers Weekly

From the towers of Manhattan to the jungles of
South America, from the sands of the Sahara to the
frozen crags of Antarctica, one man finds adventure
everywhere he goes: Gabriel Hunt.

Backed by the resources of the $100 million Hunt
Foundation and armed with his trusty Colt revolver,
Gabriel Hunt has always been ready for anything—but is
he prepared for the adventures that lie in wait for him?

HUNT AT THE WELL OF ETERNITY
James Reasoner

The woman carrying the bloodstained flag seemed
desperate for help—but it was the attack that followed
that convinced Gabriel there was something here men
would kill for. And that was before he knew about the
dungeon in the Mayan ruins, or the legendary secret
hidden in the rain forest of Guatemala…

HUNT THROUGH THE CRADLE OF FEAR
Charles Ardai

When a secret chamber is discovered inside the Great
Sphinx of Egypt, its contents will lead Gabriel to a remote
Greek island, to a stone fortress in Sri Lanka… and to a
confrontation that could decide the fate of the world!

TITANBOOKS.COM

HUNT AT WORLD'S END
Nicholas Kaufmann

Three jewels, lost for centuries and scattered across the
globe, hold the secret to a device of unspeakable power,
and only Gabriel Hunt can prevent them from falling
into the hands of an ancient Hittite cult—or of a rival
bent on world domination...

HUNT BEYOND THE FROZEN FIRE
Christa Faust

Dr. Lawrence Silver vanished while researching a
mysterious phenomenon near the South Pole. His
beautiful daughter wants to know where and why—and
it's up to Gabriel Hunt to find out. But what they'll
discover at the heart of nature's most brutal climate
could change the world forever...

HUNT AMONG THE KILLERS OF MEN
David J. Schow

The warlord's men came to New York to preserve a
terrible secret—and left a dead body in their wake. Now
Gabriel Hunt is on their trail, a path that will take him to
the treacherous alleyways and rooftops of Shanghai and
a showdown with a madman out to resurrect a deadly
figure from China's past...

TITANBOOKS.COM

HARD CASE CRIME
From the authors of GABRIEL HUNT

FIFTY-TO-ONE
Charles Ardai

After publishing a supposed non-fiction account of a heist at a Mob-run nightclub, our hero is about to learn that reading and writing pulp novels is a lot more fun than living them...

GUN WORK
David J. Schow

Life isn't always cheap south of the border—the Mexican kidnapping cartel was demanding a million dollars for Carl's wife. It was time to call in some favors. Because some situations call for negotiation, but some... call for gun work.

MONEY SHOT
Christa Faust

It all began with the phone call asking former porn star Angel Dare to do one more movie. Before she knew it, she'd been shot and left for dead. She'll get to the bottom of what's been done to her even if she has to leave a trail of bodies along the way...

CHOKE HOLD
Christa Faust

Angel Dare went into Witness Protection to escape her past But when a former co-star is gunned down, it's up to Angel to get his son safely through the Arizona desert, shady Mexican bordertowns, and the neon mirage of Las Vegas...

HARD CASE CRIME
From Mickey Spillane & Max Allan Collins

THE CONSUMMATA
Mickey Spillane & Max Allan Collins

Compared to the $40 million the cops think he stole, $75,000 may not sound like much. But it's all the money in the world to the Cuban exiles who rescued Morgan the Raider. So when it's stolen, Morgan sets out to get it back.

DEAD STREET
Mickey Spillane

For 20 years, former NYPD cop Jack Stang has lived with the memory of his girlfriend's death. But what if she weren't actually dead? Now Jack has a second chance to save the only woman he ever loved—or to lose her for good…

DEADLY BELOVED
Max Allan Collins

Marcy Addwatter killed her husband—there's no question about that. But where the cops might see an open-and-shut case, private eye Michael Tree—*Ms.* Michael Tree—sees a conspiracy. Digging into it could mean digging her own grave… and digging up her own murdered husband's…

SEDUCTION OF THE INNOCENT
Max Allan Collins

Comics are corrupting America's youth. Or so Dr. Werner Frederick would have people believe. When the crusade provokes a murder, Jack Starr—comics syndicate troubleshooter—has no shortage of suspects.

TITANBOOKS.COM

HARD CASE CRIME
From Donald E. Westlake

THE COMEDY IS FINISHED

1977: America is getting over Vietnam. But not aging
comedian Koo Davis. And not the remaining members of
the People's Revolutionary Army, who've decided that a
kidnapping would bring their cause back to life…

THE CUTIE

A rich man's mistress was dead, and the cops were
hunting for the punk accused of killing her. But he was
innocent, set up by some cutie who was too clever by
half. My job? Find the cutie—before the cutie found me.

361

The men in the tan-and-cream Chrysler came with guns
blazing. When Ray Kelly woke up in the hospital, it was
a month later, he was missing an eye, and his father was
dead. Then things started to get bad.

MEMORY

Hospitalized after a liaison with another man's wife ends
in violence, Paul Cole needs to rebuild his shattered life.
But with his memory damaged, the police hounding him,
and no way even to get home, Paul's facing steep odds…

SOMEBODY OWES ME MONEY

Cab driver Chet Conway got a great racing tip from a fare,
but when he went to get his money, he found his bookie
lying dead. Now there are cops and criminals after him,
not to mention the dead man's sister, out for revenge…

HARD CASE CRIME
From Michael Crichton writing as John Lange

ODDS ON

The plan: to rob the Reina, a super-luxury hotel. The crew: three seasoned criminals. The edge: every aspect of the scheme has been simulated in a computer, down to the last variable. The complication: three beautiful women with agendas of their own—and the sort of variables no computer can fathom…

SCRATCH ONE

To prevent an arms shipment from reaching the Middle East, a terrorist group has been carrying out targeted assassinations. In response, the US sends one of its deadliest agents to take the killers down. But when the agent is delayed in transit, lawyer Roger Carr gets mistaken for him. Will he survive long enough to prove his identity?

EASY GO

Beneath the Egyptian desert lies treasure beyond imagining. And when a professor of archaeology finds clues to the location of a Pharaoh's lost tomb, he hatches a plan to find the burial site—and plunder it. But can a five-man team of smugglers and thieves uncover what the centuries have hidden? And can they escape with it… and their lives?

ZERO COOL

Peter Ross just wanted a vacation. But when he meets the beautiful Angela Locke, he soon finds himself caught in a crossfire between rival gangs seeking a precious artifact. Ross is an ordinary man in desperate circumstances: racing to uncover a secret, before he becomes its next victim.

TITANBOOKS.COM